Children in the Attic

Children in the Attic

A.M. Overett

Children in the Attic

© A.M. Overett 2024

This book is a work of fiction. Named locations are used fictitiously, and characters and incidents are the product of the author's imagination. Any resemblance to actual events or places or persons, living or dead, is entirely coincidental.

Published by
Lighthouse Publishing
SAN 257-4330
228 Freedom Parkway
Hoschton, GA 30548
United States of America

Table of Contents

CHAPTER 1

The House on Arendelle Court

There was a house at the end of Arendelle Court that rose above the rest of the houses in the cul-de-sac, set apart and appearing haughty toward its neighbors. It was a Victorian style house that was dark and bleak and needing much tending to but the owners seemed little interested in maintenance. Eventually they sold the house to a young couple.

The couple had the house inspected before the sale and there were no outstanding issues other than a radon alert to which they would pay to have work done that would allow safe passage of the noxious gas away from the structure. On the day of the closing the couple met with the original owners and their realtor to sign the paperwork.

"Did you own the house for very long?" asked Jayne Royalton to one of the owners.

"About five years," said the man.

"I had the impression it had been in your family for years?"

"Not sure where you got that idea. We bought it at auction."

"Auction?"

"Oh yes," said the man's wife. She continued, "We had been looking for some fixer-uppers and had found out about this online. We like to flip houses."

The young couple looked at the older couple with puzzlement. Clearly the house hadn't been fixed up and as typically done with that type of investment been resold within a year.

"Well, we ended up buying another house around that period that took a lot of our time…"

"And money," the woman interrupted with a cheery smile.

The young couple looked and each other and began to wonder if what they were doing was a good idea. They had fallen in love with the home and although quite old, felt they could give it the love and attention it deserved. Charles "Charlie" Royalton was an engineer at a local construction company and Jayne Royalton was a professor of Biology at nearby South-Central State University. Both made a substantial income and thought the house to be a great project that they could either fix up and sell or keep as their own long-term home. Besides the home, the large plot of land the property was built on was close to a large forest and a big field where their children could play. Their children; Jake 16, Mikaela 10 and Zachary 8, would all have a marvelous time exploring the grounds. It was an ideal situation and the couple, although slightly concerned about the home's history, decided to go with their emotions and buy the home.

"Do you know anything about the previous owners?" Charlie asked.

"No, like we said we bought it at auction. These are typically sales resulting in the previous buyer not being able to keep up with the payments or perhaps because of criminal reasons; selling drugs, not paying their taxes and then having the property seized. It was a quickly advertised auction by the county and there was hardly anyone there so we got a great deal."

The transaction was quickly completed and the Royalton's were presented with the keys to the house. They knew they had a lot of work ahead but they felt it would be a good investment once the house was renovated. In the meantime the kids had plenty to explore and explore they did.

******

The Royalton family moved in the following weekend and although they had the money to pay someone else to do it, Charlie decided he would rent a U-Haul and save the expense. He thought it might also be a way to reconnect with Jake. Jake had become a little isolated from his parents as of late. As most teenagers do, they become a little moody as they transition between child and adult. Jake was no exception and felt he was an adult now and didn't need his parents butting into his business. Charlie and Jayne attributed his ups and downs to "just being a teenager" and felt it would soon pass. They had tried to be active in his life; getting him involved in boy scouts, guitar and sports. He had taken to soccer at an early age but recently had lost interest and they were searching for something else that might give him some purpose and drive besides school. They had also become concerned with some of the friends he was beginning to hang out with and wished he had better taste in those he associated with. Charlie vowed to Jayne he would work on getting more involved in Jake's life, much to Jake's chagrin.

Mikaela and Zachary on the other hand were much less a worry to their parents. The two were inseparable and were seldom spotted outside of each other's company. Jake isolated himself from his younger siblings so the two just made the best of it and set out on their own adventures together. Although they had friends in school, they couldn't wait to get home each day, do their homework and then run outside to play together. It was an unusually close relationship for a brother and sister.

The day the Royalton's moved into the house, Mikaela and Zachary began to run around the yard and the house. They made a half-hearted attempt at helping and were soon out of sight. They had picked out their rooms and moved all of their clothes and toys inside. Once the task was completed they spotted a stairway which piqued their curiosity. They slowly ascended the stairway and came to a door. They played with the handle which seemed very loose and covered with dust. Had their parents examined this part of the house? It looked like it hadn't been disturbed in years. They wiggled the doorknob slowly to the right and they could hear a click. They then slowly pushed the door open. The opening of the door sent a lot of dust flying into the air, causing the children to quickly cover their nose and mouth. The room was dark but they could see there were two massive ceiling windows that had been covered with what appeared to be wallpaper. The paper was thin enough so that it was able to allow faint sunlight to illuminate the room. There were all kinds of furniture throughout the attic. A lot of it had been covered with sheets. There was dust and cobwebs everywhere. As they walked they could hear the creaking of the floorboards. It was a little spooky, but Mikaela and Zachary liked spooky. Their main goal in life was to find as many adventures as possible. Here was another opportunity. Before they could finish exploring, their mother yelled up to them to come down for lunch. They sighed but complied with their mother's wishes.

After lunch Charlie asked Jake if he would help him assemble a work bench in the garage in hopes of striking up a conversation.

"So do you think you'll like the new neighborhood?" Charlie asked, hoping for any kind of audible reply.

"Looks okay I guess."

"Once we're all settled in how 'bout we sign you up for soccer again?"

"Nah, I'm tired of soccer."

"How about guitar?"

"Maybe."

Charlie pulled Jake aside and lowered his voice.

"Jake, I know you're going through some things right now but I really want you to know that you can talk to me…about anything. Whatever's on your mind I want you to be able to come to me and talk. Sex…girls…whatever you want to talk about I want you to know I am here for you."

Jake raised his eyebrow at the thought of speaking to his dad about anything like sex. He wasn't opposed to the idea but was just not feeling comfortable about opening up at that moment. He nodded to his father and gave a faint smile. His dad then patted him on the shoulder hoping that his son would know how much he wanted to connect with him. For now their little conversation would have to suffice.

After the Royaltons had settled into their home, life was slowly getting back to normal. Charlie and Jayne worked extensively on the house during the weekends, in between taking the kids to soccer matches. For his father, Jake had decided to give soccer one more season, but it was clear that it was becoming too much of a routine and his performance was more and more lethargic. Charlie had hoped that at least Jake would earn a soccer scholarship to a division 1 school, but that was becoming more and more unlikely. As his father pushed him more and more, he became less and less interested. His grades started to suffer and he was no longer routinely coming home right after school. He would tell his parents that he was "hanging out with some friends." When his parents questioned him about his friends he would become almost inaudible. Jayne would also notice that some days he seemed disheveled and his eyes looked red and glassy. Clearly something was up.

A concerned Jayne did a little research and was convinced that her son was using marijuana. When she confronted him on the issue he just shrugged and went to his room. When she followed him he would slam the door shut.

"Jake, I want to talk to you."

"I don't want to talk to you!"

Jayne would lean on the door and dream of a time when her son was more innocent and not affected by all of the turmoil of the world. Her plan was to try and find out who he was hanging out with and see if she could somehow intervene. She knew however that any intervention might create even more problems given his moody disposition as of late. His hormones were wreaking havoc so she would have to navigate cautiously.

As far as the two younger kids were concerned, they couldn't be more content. They were happy in school, always did their homework and couldn't wait for the weekends where they could play in the backyard as well as play on their soccer teams. Of course they were young and Charlie and Jayne were bracing for when they became teenagers.

CHAPTER 2

Meeting the Black Knights

Mikaela Royalton was an exceptional girl. She was a born leader and her younger brother followed her everywhere. From an early age she showed a strong intellect, much like her mother. She seemed to excel at everything she did; math, science, art, music, athletics, there was nothing she wouldn't try. Sometimes the accomplishments and attention she received rubbed Jake the wrong way, and it was another reason that he began to slowly slip away from the family, if not physically certainly emotionally.

Another strength of Mikaela's was her confidence and sociability. She made friends with everyone. She especially liked to reach out to those that seemed ostracized or seemed to be on the fringes of school society. One day at school she noticed a girl sitting alone in the cafeteria during lunch. She invited the girl over to sit with her and her friends.

"Are you sure? I'm just in the 3rd grade," the young girl asked.

"It doesn't matter to me what grade you're in. You look all alone over there. Come sit with us."

The girl picked-up her tray and complied with Mikaela's command. Mikaela introduced "Greta" to the rest of the group. Greta had a slight accent and explained that she was from Germany. Her father had recently received a position as professor of computer science at the same university that Mikaela's mother Jayne worked.

"You have an amazing grasp of English," one of the girls commented.

"Yes. I've watched a lot of American TV since I was very young. I love Disney!"

The girls chuckled at Greta's cuteness, but all secretly agreed to themselves, having also grown-up on a steady diet of Frozen, Beauty and the Beast and the Lion King.

"Do you play any sports Greta?" Mattie, Mikaela's "official BFF" asked.

"I play a little soccer."

"That's great! You can maybe play on my little sister's team. She's also in the 3rd grade. We all play at the Penn Academy. You should sign up."

"Being from Germany you must be pretty good?" Mikaela asked.

"Well, I don't play a lot. My dad played a lot of soccer back in Germany and he used to teach me things, but I'm not very good."

"What else do you like to do?"

"I like to read." She pulled a book up from her bag and showed it to the other girls.

"Wow, you read *Lord of the Rings*? That looks like a long book!" Brittany Ryan said with a look of semi-disgust.

"No, I love it. I read most of Tolkien's books. I'm just reading this again for fun."

"For fun! What kind of looney are you?!!!" Brittany said practically yelling.

"Calm down Brittany. Just because you can barely get through Captain Underpants, doesn't mean you have to put down Greta," Mikaela said putting her hand on Greta's shoulder.

"Very funny Mickey!"

Greta had a puzzled look on her face, "Mickey? Like Mickey Mouse?"

"Yeah, my so-called 'friends' call me Mickey. You can call me Mickey or Mikey or Mikaela…whatever you like."

Greta smiled a bright profound smile. A look like she had truly been comforted by Mikaela. The girls continued their conversation and learned much about Greta. She seemed to have had a very interesting life back in Germany. Mikaela, although thinking Greta quite young, felt she could be a good friend to her. The girls finished their food just in time for the bell to ring, signaling time to return to class.

"Great meeting you Greta! Hope you have a great day!" Mikaela said as she quickly gathered her bag and tray and headed toward the exit of the cafeteria. Greta smiled and waved as the girls soon ran out of sight. She breathed a sigh of relief, thankful that she now had some friends and could possibly integrate into her new environment.

Later that day, across town at Benjamin Franklin High School, the bell had rung for the day and kids were either heading for the buses or walking home, with the exception of Jake Royalton who was meeting several of his friends in a nearby hideout in the woods. Jake was excited to be rid of his confinement. He felt like he was on the fringes of society, a type of outlaw and it thrilled him. His life as a suburban child who always obeyed his parents was over. He was now a man, or at least that was what he thought he was. Puberty was not a sign of instant manhood, but for Jake it was. He didn't need any direction from anyone, he was his own man. And for all human beings entering adolescence and beyond, isn't that the truth? We feel we know it all. We don't need the rules of God or parent to tell us what to do. We know it all. Whether a wealthy investor, a state senator, or a janitor, we humans know it all and we shouldn't be told what to do, or so we believe.

As Jake entered the woods, which was a part of the Jefferson Township Nature Reserve, he felt like he was on a mission. A mission to outwit society and more specifically, his parents. He walked about a quarter mile through the forest. It seemed to get darker and darker as he stepped through. He had only been to the "hideout" once before. He eventually saw a small clearing and could hear a few voices. As he neared his friends he could hear them talking about various teachers in school. As he tread on a branch he was met with a loud response…

"Halt who goes there?!!!" yelled his friend Mac. Macintosh McNabb was the ringleader of their little group. Sometimes known as "Mac" or "McMac", he was the self-ordained leader of the Black Knights and the "world's greatest rapper," which was subject to ridicule by everyone around including the members of the Black Knights.

Jake could see the boys had already been smoking pot and were engaged in their usual conversations about the world.

"Why do you think Knights start with a K?" Will Staton asked as he took a hit from the pipe that was going around.

"Oh, hey Jake, come on in," Breck Wilson waved to Jake to move into their little gathering.

The hideout, also known as "basecamp" was a small crater created by an old oak tree that had collapsed. Within the crater were multiple bricks of varying sizes that had been assembled into makeshift furniture. Most of the bricks were concrete blocks they had stolen from different construction sites. With the bricks and blocks they had constructed a fire pit, and four chairs. They had also stolen multiple 2 x 4's they used to create the chairs by sticking them into the holes of the concrete blocks. Probably the most prized piece of furniture was a makeshift table they had made out of the blocks that served as the storage for their stash and where the paraphernalia was kept.

As Jake entered the sanctum he was handed the pipe which he quickly took a hit from. He had only smoked pot a couple of times previously, which his mother had caught him both times. He breathed a deep breath and was immediately feeling the stress leave his body. A few hits more and he was ready to lead the charge on Normandy Beach, he felt so elated.

The conversation was also quite stimulating; "Was their life on Mars?" "Was there life in the old abandon house down the street?" "What were Twix candy bars really made of?" "Do dolphins cry?" "Would the Dolphins win the Super Bowl?" "How far was the end of the Universe?" "Were Katie Perkin's boobs real?" The debates went on and on with Jake laughing but seldom contributing to the conversations. He was in state of complete bliss and ecstasy. He could feel the stress oozing from his body. But why did a sixteen-year-old boy have so much stress? Was it the expectations of his parents to succeed? Was it the daily grind of having to go to school? Was it the need to constantly find friends and fit in? For Jake, and all high school kids it was the same; trying to figure out the world and what was their place in it.

After several hours of the boys smoking pot and deciding how they would take over the world, they decided it was time to go home.

"Boy, I hope it's not too late. I lose all track of time when I am high. My dad will kill me if I am too late," Mac said in a concerned voice.

"C'mon, it's not like he's going to hit you are something," Breck said, soon realizing what the truth was.

"Ok boys, let's sing our club song and then hit the road!"

The boys stood up and began to chant, with Jake just mouthing the words…

We the Black Knights, of great courage and power

Vow to meet each week at this very same hour

*We pledge to one another to keep this
sacred bond*
*To not let the world break our friendship so
fond*
*And when our teachers and parents have a
fit*
We can go tell the world to go fuck it!

The boys then gave each other a salute
which ended with them placing their hands in the
middle and then raising them as if their hands were
birds flying away. Breck quickly extinguished the
fire that they had made and they all bolted off in
four different directions. Jake had a big goofy
smile on his face as he ran all the way home.
Although experiencing euphoria at that moment,
he knew it would quickly subside when he was
greeted by his parents.

When Jake arrived home, he felt completely
out of it as he tried to relate to his family who
seemed to him almost cartoonish in their world of
domesticity. He was offered dinner but ran up to
his room.

"Jake, you need to have dinner!" his mother
yelled to him as he ran up the stairs.

"I'm not hungry!" He was actually starving
but his mood was so buoyant that he could wait
until later to come down and raid the pantry.

The rest of the family stared at each other wondering what was going on with Jake. It was clear to Charlie and Jayne that they would have to do something but what? For Charlie the answer was clear. Jake would have to stop meeting with his friends. He would need to be grounded until he could get his grades up. Now, how would he communicate that message? With a loud pronouncement or a soft, drawn out negotiation?

Upstairs, Jake lied in his bed with a Playboy magazine he had been given by one of his friends. He used to look at porn on his smart phone and tablet until his parents took those away. He was almost seventeen and the pressure to have sex was becoming stressful. In many ways he wondered what it was like and would it be fun. At other times he thought he was too young and he should just focus on being a kid; playing soccer and just hang out with friends, friends other than those in the "hideout".

"Jake," his mother said softly through the door, sending Jake into a panic. He flung the magazine into the closet.

"I'm tired mom, I don't want to talk now."

"It might help if you talk to me."

Jayne leaned on the door hoping that Jake would relent. She stood there for several minutes waiting for a reply.

"I don't want to talk to you mom, I'm tired. Maybe some other time."

Jayne sighed, nodded and then walked back downstairs. She was struggling with the emotional distance she felt between her and her son. She wondered if they would ever have the relationship they once did.

CHAPTER 3

An Unexpected Guest

The following Saturday, the Royaltons went to work on the house. The entire family including the now grounded Jake began clearing out the attic. The house which had been built in 1896 was of a Victorian style and had gone through several renovations. It had two floors plus an attic and a basement. The basement was going to be a lot of work but for now the furnace was fine and so Charlie was going to save that for last. As they entered the attic they were immediately greeted with a musty odor. During their inspection, they had taken a quick look to make sure there were no structural issues but had left it the same way they had found it. There were multiple pieces of furniture that had been covered with cloths. There was a full-length mirror and a vintage sewing machine that if fixed up might be worth something. The couple that they had purchased the house from said they had not touched the items in the attic and had left it as is. No one wanted to take the trouble to dispose of the various items.

What was interesting about the attic was that it had been renovated in the 1920s, with the owner adding large windows to the ceiling. During the middle of the summer when the Earth was at its closest axis toward the sun, the sunshine would beam down into the room and bath everything in light. The previous owners surmised that it might have been an attempt to create some sort of green house or possibly better light for an art studio. They were unsure though as to why the windows had been covered up with what appeared to be wallpaper. Also added was a small loft that looked like it could be used as a small bedroom. There was no bed there so they were not sure what the original intent was.

The first point of order was to move all the furniture to one corner and then clear the entire place of dust. Mikaela and Zachary grabbed a couple of brooms and began to sweep up the floor, much to Jayne's annoyance as she received a healthy dose of dusty air into her face. She was practically choking on the dust but was eventually revived. She gave her children a mock frown and then motioned for them to continue. Jayne instructed Jake to wipe down the walls with a bucket of soapy water and sponge. Charlie inspected a floorboard that was slowly disintegrating and began plans to replace it. Jayne began to go through the furniture to see if anything could be salvaged. She removed the various cloths and was impressed with a few of the pieces. They looked like they might be valuable antiques. Since the entire home was antique, she wanted the inside to have more of modern feel. She began plans to remove the pieces and to take them to town and sell them. Once Jake had completed cleaning the walls, he and his siblings were elected to help take the furniture down to the living room. Charlie helped Jake with the larger pieces while Mikaela and Zachary took down the various lamps, stools, nightstands and other nick knacks. By the late afternoon the room had been completely cleared and cleaned. The kids were exhausted and collapsed on the sofa in the living room to watch a little TV. Charlie ordered pizza and later the family played boardgames. Jake was half engaged which for Charlie and Jayne was a good sign. He might not be all there, but half of Jake was better than no Jake.

"So do you think you'll try out for JV next year Jake?" his father asked.

"I don't know. Maybe."

"What else you going to do?"

"I was thinking maybe taking guitar lessons."

"That would be great!" said Jayne, practically yelling with enthusiasm. She wanted her son preoccupied with something other than hanging out with his friends.

"There's a music school downtown. We can sign you up on Monday when I get off of work," Jayne offered.

Jake shrugged his shoulders as if agreeing to the idea.

"Yes, you used to be one of the best air-guitarists I had ever seen!" Mikaela said with some sincerity. Zachary giggled. Jake ignored her. For the past year Jake and Mikaela's relationship had been strained. Jake had started to feel inferior to his younger sister. She was smart, talented and had a great personality. All things that Jake felt he wasn't. As for Zachary, he was practically non-existent to his older brother. Jake had little authority over Zachary as Zachary obeyed everything his sister told him to do.

****

The following weekend Mikaela and Zachary had an out-of-town soccer tournament and so the house belonged to Charlie and Jake. The father and son would start working on the basement. The only way to describe the basement was it was black. Charlie assumed that it was from the original coal burning furnace. There was an old wooden workbench and a few pieces of furniture but apart from that the basement was not cluttered. Charlie inspected the furnace which had been replaced within the last five years. He brought in a dehumidifier and a large lamp so they could review the foundation and the floor better. Jake began cleaning the brick foundation with his now familiar bucket of sudsy water and sponge. He marveled at the thick black soot that adhered to the bricks.

Charlie moved the various pieces of furniture to the first floor so they could clear things out. At around noon, Charlie volunteered to go get sandwiches for lunch. He asked Jake to continue cleaning which he did for another five minutes. Jake's attention at been caught by a small room that was toward the far end of the basement. He wondered what was inside and walked over to the doorway. He turned the knob and slowly tried to push the door open. There seemed to be something blocking the door. He grabbed a flashlight and tried to peer inside. He could see it was a large cardboard box. He pushed harder and soon was inside. There were two large metal shelving units for storage with various boxes on them. He walked to the far end of the room, wanting to inspect what was on the other end of the shelving units.

As he approached what appeared to be the back of the room, he could see a string dangling from the ceiling. He pulled on it and a light bulb above him turned on. As the light went on he jumped with fright. There was a girl standing there. She immediately grabbed one of his wrists to pull him closer. She then clamped her hand firmly over his mouth.

"Don't be scared. I won't hurt you."

The girl looked to be in her late teens. She had curly blonde shoulder length hair that had been tied back. She was wearing a school uniform, with a white blouse and plaid skirt. Jake assumed she was a student from St. Pius catholic high school.

"If you promise not to call for help, I'll remove my hand."

The wide-eyed Jake, who was slowly calming down, nodded his head in compliance.

"Who are you?"

"I'm Stella."

"Why are you here?"

"I live here."

"You live here? But we live here."

"Yes, but I was here before you."

"Yes but my parents purchased the house."

"Look, I'm hiding from my parents. They are horrible. They have been abusing me so I ran away from home a couple of months ago and this place was open so I have been hiding here."

Jake inspected Stella noting that it looked like she hadn't bathed in a while. She had smudges on her face and legs which he couldn't tell were from dirt or possibly part of the "abuse" she was talking about.

"Have you been eating?"

"Yes, I sneak up at night to the kitchen and take food. Before you guys came I had a friend give me some food."

"Why don't you just report your parents to the police?"

As Jake finished his sentence they could hear that his father had returned home and was walking around in the kitchen. Stella again placed her hand over Jake's mouth and raised her index finger to her lips.

"Please don't tell your family I am down here. I just need some time to figure out what I'm going to do," she whispered.

Jake was confused. What should he do? Clearly she looked like she needed help. He nodded silently and she smiled that he had acquiesced to her request.

"Thank you," she said removing her hand from his mouth.

"My dad will probably find you here," he said in a whisper.

"I'll go out the storm door. Just make sure it's not locked when I come back."

He nodded again in compliance. As he searched around the room, in one corner he could see there was a cot made up with several blankets and a pillow. On the other corner there were steps leading up to the storm door that she had mentioned.

"Isn't the door locked?" he questioned, having seen the storm door from the outside.

"I picked it with a hairpin."

"But how did you replace it once you were inside."

"The doors don't close tightly. The bracket is loose and so I can stick my hands outside to access the lock. Before you guys came I usually left it unlocked."

Stella smiled at Jake and walked up to him. She gave him a smile and looked deeply into his eyes. He had never dated much and had been intimated by girls. There had been pressure as he grew up to no longer be a virgin, especially from his friends but had never really looked to have a girlfriend – it just looked like too much work. She grabbed his shirt and pulled him into her. She gave him a long peck on the cheek. His heart was pounding and he was starting to feel aroused.

"So what's your name?"

"Jake."

"Well Jakey boy, remember, please keep our little secret," she said with a coy smile. He nodded. She turned and walked up the stairs to the storm door. He looked closely at her, enjoying her feminine form as she ascended the stairs. She was soon gone and he could hear his father coming down from the kitchen.

******

To avoid the stress of the new move and the moodiness of Jake, Mikaela and Zachary would often go out to the fields in the backyard to get away from everything. There they would play; climbing trees, throwing rocks into a nearby brook and looking for buried treasure. It was also a time when the two siblings would simply lie down in the tall grass and talk. They would look up into the sky and look for different cloud shapes. They would giggle and laugh at the outrageous figures they would see.

"What do you think is going on with Jake?" Zachary asked.

"I don't know. I hear that he is entering puberty. Not sure what that is, but he's always moody.

"Maybe we can cheer him up...like a party or something."

"That's a great idea!"

Before they could speak another word their privacy was interrupted. A shadow caught Mikaela's eye.

"Hello. What are you guys doing?"

"Hey Greta! What are you doing here?"

"My house is over there." Greta pointed to a group of trees to the west. A structure could be seen if you looked closely.

"Wow, that's great. I didn't know you lived so close. Do you want to hang out?"

"Sure."

The brother and sister invited Greta to their house. As they entered the front door and ran into the kitchen they greeted their mother with a hug.

"Mom, this is Greta. She lives at the end of the field at the back of our house. She goes to our school."

"Well hello Greta, it's nice to meet you." Jayne said bending slightly to shake Greta's hand.

"Nice to meet you Mrs. Royalton," Greta said with a bright smile that cheered Jayne.

"Why don't you all go play for a bit and I'll make some cookies."

The kids shrieked with delight and then headed up to Mikaela's bedroom. Mikaela proudly showed off her room to Greta hoping she would be duly impressed. While disregarding Mikaela's toys and various electronic media devices, Greta was drawn to pictures of Mikaela's family, especially a Christmas family photo of the entire family from a couple of years prior. The family looked so happy together, even Jake who had not yet experienced the pangs of puberty.

"Do you have any more?"

"More what?"

"Photos of your family."

Puzzled by the request, Mikaela showed Greta a stack of photo albums that were in her closet.

"My mom's a bit old school. She should keep all this stuff on our computer. She won't even let me have a phone so I can take my own photos."

"Well, it's good, kids spend way too much time on their phones and social media."

Mikaela gave Greta a look of surprise. It was exactly something her mother would say to her. Greta sat crossed legged on the floor of Mikaela's closet and poured herself over the photo albums. She smiled with glee at the various ages of the kids and laughed at the funny antics they would sometimes get into. After twenty minutes of Greta's review, Mikaela suggested they do something else to which Greta complied.

"Hey, I noticed a stairway at the end of the hall, can we go up there?" Greta asked. Mikaela nodded somewhat hesitantly. She had only been up there once and practically died of dust inhalation. Her mother had been working on the attic for the past several weeks so she was curious on the progress.

After escorting Greta and Zachary up the stairs, she slowly pushed the door to the attic open. As she opened it she was surprised to see all the work her mother had put into it. It was completely clean with a fresh coat of paint on the walls. There was a rocking chair, an armoire, a small bed with a nightstand and lamp and a large desk with a computer.

"I think my mom wants to make this her office."

"Wow, it looks awesome," Greta said.

The trio slowly walked through the attic noting how nice and organized it was. They laughed that this could be their new hideout. Much of the attic, which extended the full length of the house, had open space where they could add their own toys and maybe even create a game room.

"Wow look at those large ceiling windows. I bet they would add a lot of light if you removed that paper."

"I don't think my mom's gotten around to it yet."

"Hey kids, the cookies are ready!" Jayne could be heard from downstairs. The kids immediately dropped what they were doing and ran downstairs for their treat.

"Only two cookies, I don't want you spoiling your dinner."

Mikaela grabbed some milk from the refrigerator and poured three glasses to which she quickly moved over to the kitchen table, spilling some of its contents in her haste.

"Mikaela! Watch what you're doing!"

"Sorry mom."

As the kids chomped down on their cookies like homeless waifs who had never seen such treats, Charlie walked through the front door and into the kitchen. The kids ran over and gave him a hug and then quickly ran back to finish their cookies.

"Hi dear," he said, giving Jayne a peck on the cheek.

"Hi hon, how was your day?"

"Good, a lot of long meetings but we got a lot accomplished."

"Hey dad, this is Greta!" Mikaela quickly blurted before inhaling the rest of her cookie.

"Nice to meet Greta. Are you new to our fair town?"

"Yes sir. My dad is a professor of IT at the university."

"What's his name?"

"Uh, Gustav Bierman."

There was a slight pause in Greta's voice which made the couple question her truthfulness. Maybe she wasn't used to saying her father's first name, after all, children always use a term of endearment for their parents.

"Well welcome Greta. I hope you and your family enjoy it here."

"Oh, I'm sure we will."

"Greta, let's go back up in the attic. Maybe we can create a place for my barbies."

"Just make sure you keep out of my stuff while you're up there," Jayne yelled as the three friends ran out of the kitchen.

"So how was your day dear?" Charlie asked as he looked at a pot of boiling chicken soup on the range.

"Good. I was feeling a little fatigue today."

"You're probably overdoing it again," Charlie said as he grabbed her and pulled her in to his body. He gave her a long kiss on the lips to which she smiled a coy smile.

"You're in a good mood."

"I am. I finally feel like I am getting somewhere with my department. I think we now have the funds we need and to put together attractive proposals for our clients."

"That is good news."

As they renewed their romantic embrace, Jake came in from the backdoor of the kitchen.

"Hey buddy, want to shoot some hoops?"

"Nah, got some homework."

Although the same moody kid, Charlie and Jayne were at least glad he was coming home promptly every day. What they didn't realize was that Jake had a new interest in being at home and especially in the basement.

Later that night when everybody was in bed, Jake snuck down to the kitchen. He made a salami sandwich with potato chips and a glass of milk to which he took down to the basement on a tray. He negotiated his way to the back room as the basement had now become the storage place for all the extra furniture and odds and ends. He wrapped lightly on the door and Stella quickly appeared. She looked more beautiful than ever. She was now wearing a bathrobe and looked like she had recently bathed. She explained to Jake that she had taken a shower while everyone had been out of the house.

"You look great," Jake said in a shy and reserved voice.

"Thank you. You too. That sandwich looks good."

She opened the door and Jake walked in. The room looked a little more decorated than before.

"I hope you don't mind but I took some of your parent's furniture to fix up the room a bit."

"I think for now it's fine. They've just thrown a bunch of their stuff down here for the time being. I don't think they have any plans to move it for a while. At least until they get the upstairs fixed-up."

Stella smiled, appreciating Jake's understanding.

"You can join me on the bed while I eat this great looking sandwich."

Stella plopped down with the tray and immediately patted her hand on the bed to invite Jake to join her.

"So tell me about yourself?"

Jake was a little nervous. He had not really been alone with a girl before, especially one so beautiful and mature. Being at an awkward age it was difficult for him to be himself with anyone, let alone a girl so attractive.

"Um, well, as you know my name's Jake, I'm sixteen…"

"Sixteen? You look so mature Jake," she said with a coy smile.

"How old are you?"

"I'm seventeen," she said twisting a strand of her curly blonde hair in a very seductive and sensual way. She then chomped down hard on her sandwich as if she were an animal tearing into her prey. Something that Jake took as a metaphor in their current situation.

"Jake? Is that short for Jacob?"

"Yes."

"Then I will call you Jacob."

Although not in love with the name Jacob, he would comply with most anything the girl would order him to do.

"No, on second thought, I think I'll just call you Jakey. And as you are aware my name's Stella. Stella North."

Jake nodded, staring at the way she then gulped down the entire glass of milk in one go. He was duly impressed.

"Stand up Jakey," she ordered her submissive male. Jake complied and wondered what she wanted. Jake's eyes began to wander around the room in an uncomfortable manner. What should he do? What would his parents do if they found him alone with a girl?

"Ok…"

"Turn around. I want to take a good look at you."

Jake slowly and awkwardly turned around as Stella bit her lip in a provocative way. He had no clue what she was doing.

"Very good. You have a nice build. You look sturdy and athletic."

Jake was confused by her comments. She seemed to be sizing him up for something. Did she want to have sex with him?

"Now lie on the bed," Stella stood up and motioned for him to lie down on the bed. Jake laid himself on the bed wondering what was coming next. He had never been with a girl and was not exactly sure how it all worked. She then pulled a backpack from underneath the bed and took out some papers from it. On closer inspection they appeared to be sketches.

"You would make a marvelous model for me Jakey," she said as she laid down next to him to show her artwork. Jake began to breath hard, not sure if he should take some sort of romantic action. He had watched men in movies and TV be bold and kiss the women they were with. But was that something he should do? Would she want him to do that? Would it be an act of rape? He had heard all kinds of stories about the MeToo movement and how women were speaking out about sexual assault and sexual abuse by men. With that thought he was content just to lie near her. She smelt beautiful.

For the rest of the night the two talked about their lives and their dreams. Jake was surprised by how cultured Stella was – she seemed to know everything about art, literature, politics and history. The eventual question came which was how long did she intend to stay in the basement? To which she shrugged and then rolled over and gave him a passionate kiss. She then instructed Jake to go back up to his room. Her wish was his command. He would do anything for her. She gave him a goodbye peck on the cheek and escorted him to the door. She closed the door tight, whispering something incoherent. Jake was on cloud 9 or 10 or 100, he didn't quite know, but at that moment he did not care about anything. He was happy and content and did not want the feeling to end. He looked at the door and vowed to make Stella his wife. As he walked back up the stairs he realized it was a ridiculous notion as he was only sixteen. He had to graduate high school first, but after that he was going to wed her.

CHAPTER 4

The Portal of Light

The relationship between the three friends; Greta, Mikaela and Zachary began to settle into an almost daily routine. Jayne was fine with it as long as they finished their homework first. When homework was completed and snacks consumed, the trio would religiously go to the attic where they would use a large doll house that Charlie had built as their source of make-believe, pretending they were in another time, fighting dragons and foiling ogres. Jayne would work at her desk while the imagined mayhem reigned nearby.

As the next several months went by and the children's routine continued, they noticed their mother was becoming less and less engaged in their activities. She was spending more time in the kitchen and their father seemed to be coming home more and more earlier. On the weekends it was only their father taking them to their soccer games with Jayne making a periodic showing.

One day, after coming home from school, Mikaela, Greta and Zachary noticed Jayne in the kitchen crying. Charlie was home and sitting with her holding her hands.

"Mom, what is it?" Mikaela said rushing to her side.

Charlie immediately gathered the kids and moved them over to the family room. As he did so, Jake entered the through the front door and was instructed by his father to join them on the family room sofa.

"Ah, I have some bad news about your mom. She received some results from the doctor today and…and well, she has cancer," Charlie said with one of his hands clearly trembling. The kids were stunned and could not believe what they were hearing.

"Are they sure?" Mikaela asked.

"Yes. They've run multiple tests and it seems pretty conclusive."

"What can be done?" Jake asked, seeming for the first time in months to be an actual part of the family.

"Well, they want to start her on chemo next week and see how she responds. Unfortunately I will be needing to take your mom to a lot of appointments and it will be difficult to take you to practice. I've asked Mrs. Miller if she can take you so starting tomorrow night the three of you will need to go with the Miller family to soccer practice."

The kids, including Greta looked like the wind had been sucked out of them. They were all in shock.

"Look, we need to be strong for mom. We all need to pull our weight around here especially as it relates to chores. We need to keep our rooms tidy, help with washing up and making dinner. Understood?"

All four nodded in unison, not sure what this meant for the future. As Charlie finished his instructions, Jayne walked into the room. All four of the children rushed to her side. Charlie joined them as they had a group hug. No words were spoken. Only sighs and sniffling could be heard. The group clutched each other tightly and trembling could be felt by each member, including Greta.

******

As time went by, Jayne began to spend more and more time in bed recovering from her chemo appointments. She eventually had to take a leave of absence from the university and her mother began to help out with the house and keeping an eye on the children. "Nanna" would let the children play up in the attic knowing it was a safe place and they would be occupied.

For the "trio" as Charlie began to refer to them as, they continued to spend time in the attic. With their mother no longer going up there they had the whole place to themselves. It became therapeutic.

"What's going to happen to mom?" Zachary asked one day.

"She's going to get better," Mikaela said unconvincingly.

"Yes she will," Greta said in a confident voice.

"She doesn't seem to be getting better though," Zachary said bowing his head to look at the gladiator doll he was holding in his lap. Greta immediately changed the subject.

"I wonder if we can peel off those pieces of wallpaper over the ceiling windows?"

Mikaela and Zachary looked skyward. Anything to take their minds off their mother's situation. The three grabbed a nearby ladder and Mikaela began the ascent to the top. She could just reach the bottom of one of the windows. She began to pry up one end of the wallpaper.

"Well, it looks like the paper is all dried up. I can easily remove it."

Mikaela removed what paper she could and then suggested they get the mop in the kitchen.

They would remove the mop head and then use the handle to pry up the rest of the paper. The paper seemed to disintegrate easily as they applied the mop handle and soon the two large ceiling windows were completely free of the covering. The sun's brilliant rays filled the attic. The room seemed different somehow, like it had been magically changed; painted or redecorated, it seemed to come to life now that the windows were no longer obscured. The children were stunned at the change and began to look around. The room seemed to pulsate with life.

"Hey look," Greta shouted as she pointed to the back wall of the attic. There appeared to be a door.

"Hmmm, I don't remember a door being there," questioned Zachary.

"Why would a door be there?"

"Maybe this place used to be a barn or something? Maybe they would shovel out hay?" Greta offered. The three children walked near to the door and could see that it was covered in wallpaper. It wasn't until the intense light that was shining from the ceiling windows was allowed in that the door was made visible.

"I don't know if we should open this, it might be dangerous and we could fall," Zachary said with alarm.

The two girls ignored him and began to pry away the wallpaper. The door which looked like one solid piece of dark oak had no doorknob. It had a small hole with a piece of rope extended through. It looked like something that you would pull that would raise a lever. They pulled on it and could hear the door creak. They began to push slowly not wanting to fall. From the attic to the ground below would be a drop of about 30 feet. As they pushed they could see light pouring through the door jam. When they pushed it all the way open they couldn't believe their eyes. Instead of the backyard to their house, there was what looked like an entire new world. It was a large expanse with clouds surrounding it. There were large green fields with incredibly tall oak trees, lakes and rivers and shimmering waterfalls.

"What is this place?" Mikaela asked stunned.

"We must be dreaming right?"

"I don't think we could be having the same dream."

"C'mon, let's go!" Zachary yelled.

"No, wait. This doesn't seem right," Mikaela cautioned holding back Zachary with her arm.

"This is a good place. There is nothing to fear," Greta said in a calming tone.

"What if we fall? The ground is too far down, we'll hurt ourselves…maybe kill ourselves!"

Greta smiled and then walked through the door. She appeared to step straight onto the clouds.

"See. There's nothing to fear."

Zachary yelped and then immediately ran through the door to join her.

"C'mon, Mickey, it's totally safe!"

Mikaela cautiously stepped onto one of the clouds and could feel her foot land on firm ground. She could not believe it. Shouldn't they be falling to the ground by the side of the house? she thought to herself. She looked at Greta and Zachary who had bright smiles on their faces. Why was she so doubtful?

"Come on Mikaela, it's totally safe," Greta said as if she had experienced all of this before.

As Mikaela walked further a warm feeling of love and self-confidence seemed to overtake her. It was like with every step she became more and more courageous and a surge of great happiness overwhelmed her.

"C'mon slowpokes, let's go."

The children ran through the clouds and were transported to emerald green fields of grass. They ran and ran like they had the energy and strength of stallions. Quickly they were upon a lake. The lake was like nothing they had seen before. It was crystalline and clear. They could see everything at the bottom; various ferns and forms of weed, fish, and turtles, all were plain to see. There was no murkiness to the water. They then walked on a path by a river that veered away from the lake. They began to run along its banks jumping over various tree roots. It was like they would float over the roots and lower branches. They screamed with joy. It was a feeling of complete freedom; free from all human constraint and rules.

They eventually arrived at a large waterfall. They looked down. It was as if it went down for miles as they could not see the bottom. They were so elated; they felt as though they could fly down the falls.

"Should we jump?"

"Won't we be killed?"

"No, it will be safe," came Greta's usual confident response.

The kids then jumped into the river right were the falls started. They immediately went over the edge and were free falling. But instead of fear they felt a wonderful sensation they had never felt before. They flew down the waterfall and finally arrived at the bottom, splashing and tumbling in the whitewash. The water was such that they could see each other clearly. They laughed and were able to talk to each other underneath the water. When speaking, they didn't choke and could hear each other clearly; there was no gurgling or muffled speech. They also could swim with the speed of dolphins. They would circle each other and then swim to the top, springing out of the water like they had large dorsal fins.

After having fun in the water they walked onto the shore and were immediately dry. They decided to walk toward a hill that was in the distance. It had a bright light shining over it giving it a sort of corona effect. After only walking a few feet they could see strange bright shapes like orbs jetting from around the back of the hill coming toward them. They looked like little flying saucers. They zoomed around the children; over their heads, around their bodies, whooshing as they went by making the children laugh. They finally assembled into a line in front of the children; there were five of them.

"Hello," one of the orbs said.

"Hi," said Mikaela mesmerized.

The creatures seemed to have human features but the light beaming from them was so bright that they couldn't exactly make out their faces. It was pretty similar to everything in this new mystical land. It was like being in a dreamlike state, yet fully aware that what they were experiencing was also reality. The other thing they noticed was that their senses were different. They no longer perceived sight, smell and sound like they did back on Earth. They could see, hear and smell everything all at once. Their sight was 360 degrees. They could hear every sound there was; birds, the wind, music, every beat and vibration and all at once. And the smells were incredible, it was like smelling every form of flower and perfume all at the same time. It was incredible. Were they in heaven? Perhaps the orbs would tell them.

"Welcome to ----------------."

"Welcome to what?" Zachary asked.

"Welcome to ----------------."

The children did not know exactly what word the orb was using. They could understand the words "Welcome to." But when the orb said the name of where they were it was like an image or a thought that entered their head. It wasn't so much a word as it was an impression. It was like the essence of where they were was placed into their minds. They had heard the words "heaven," "paradise," "nirvana," but was this a place that had no word for it? A place so wonderful that you could not name it?

The children had a warm feeling running through their souls as they stood in the presence of the orbs. They were suspended in the air and there was a rustling sound as if they had wings. Maybe they were angels?

"Who are you?" Mikaela asked.

"We are your friends!" one of them said with a lot of enthusiasm.

"My name is Elethria."

"My name is Lumina."

"My name is Gallatam.

"My name is Selebria."

"My name is Niamthan."

As each spoke their name they revealed their genders; Elethria, Lumina and Selebria were females and Gallatam and Niamthan were males. They could tell from their appearance and voices that they were either feminine or masculine.

"Are you angels?" Zachary asked.

"No. One day we hope to be angels but we are merely in training right now. Anyway we are here to serve you during your stay."

"This is a wonderful place. Is it like Earth?"

"Oh no. This is a sacred place. Earth is in decay and one day will pass."

"Not soon will it?" Zachary said concerned.

"That day we do not know. But in the meantime, you should enjoy your stay here."

"Can we get something to eat?" Mikaela asked.

"You should ask your friend here," Elethria pointed to Greta.

"Greta, you know about this place?"

Greta nodded her head. She grabbed Mikaela and Zachary by the hands and began to walk with them. She seemed to have a gleaming aura and looked different from what she normally did.

"Greta are you an angel too?"

"I hope to one day become an angel. It's up to the Great Light to decide. In any case I am happy just to be with you."

The children walked some distance through beautiful fields, valleys and forests, trying to keep up with their new friends. They followed the orbs over to what appeared to be a temple of some sort. It had a clear dome that looked like it was made of light-blue crystal. Supporting the dome were large gold and white columns. One of the orbs hovered by the children and pointed for them to enter through one of the openings between the columns. Inside was a large round stone table. It looked like it was made from the most beautiful marble or granite. On the table was a layout of all foods imaginable; fruits and vegetables, desserts, beverages of all colors, shapes and sizes, it was more of a feast for the eyes than for the stomach.

At the far end of the table there was a bright light. As the children neared the light it appeared to be a woman clothed in a radiant white gown.

"Come closer my children," the woman said in the most soothing voice imaginable. The children all took seats next to her. The seats were beautiful – the cushions looked like they were made from silk with thick padding that was so soft it was as if made from goose feathers. The legs and backrest were all trimmed with gold.

"Please eat as much as you like," she said gesturing with her hand.

"Who are you?" Mikaela asked.

"I am Queen ------------------."

Just like when the name of this world was spoken, likewise the queen's name was not pronounceable but an image in their minds appeared of peace, calm and light. It gave the children a warm feeling each time her name was mentioned. The children picked up large crystal plates and began to help themselves to all the food that was set before them. Mikaela loved the pineapple and applesauce. Zachary loved the warm, soft bread, and Greta liked everything.

"Oh, this bread is like heaven!" Zachary shouted with glee.

"I'm glad you like it Zachary."

"How do you know my name?"

"Oh, I know a lot of things."

"Really, like what?"

"What would you like to know?"

"Uh, well…"

"What is that light on the hill over there?" Mikaela jumped in, interrupting Zachary.

"That is the Great Light."

"Oh yes, I remember the…the…"

"The Guardians?"

"Is that what they are called?"

"Yes."

"What is the purpose of the Great Light?"

"The Great Light is what gives life to the universe. The universe does not exist without the Great Light. Everything that has life in it owes its existence to the Great Light."

"Wow, that's wonderful! Is it like our sun?"

"No. Your sun is a physical entity, but the Great Light is not a physical thing you can touch. It is the essence of total purity of total love and energy."

"That is awesome! This place is like heaven!" Zachary practically yelled.

"It is," Greta said matter-of-factly.

"How do you know Greta?" Mikaela asked.

"This is where I came from. I'm just visiting your world."

"What?" Zachary said in shock. But as Mikaela and Zachary started to think about it, it began to make sense. They had always known that Greta was different but did not understand that she was from another world. She was always the most calm and soothing of characters; always had a smile on her face and a nice word to say.

"I sent Greta to your world to help you. I want to give you wisdom from this world so you can help others in your world," said the queen.

"Yes your majesty," said Zachary.

"No need to call me that. You can call me Mother Light."

"Oh, I like that name. At least we can pronounce that," Mikaela laughed.

After the children finished their meals, Mother Light invited them into a large domed building that was just behind the temple. As they walked in it appeared to be a large banquet hall. It looked like it went on forever, with hundreds of tables going on as far as the eye could see, or at least the physical eye could see. At the tables were many orbs. As they walked with Mother Light by the orbs, they perceived them as people.

"This is the Great Hall children. People who used to live on Earth who have since passed now live here."

The children were fascinated. As they walked by the orbs they could now see that they were people. The people were engaged in lively debates and conversations. They looked so happy and were very friendly with each other. It made the children think that their world would be so wonderful if people could converse with each other like this; no more arguments or fighting.

As they continued to walk, the people would look at Mother Light and wave or bow to her saying hello or giving her a greeting. They began to perceive the identities of the people. Some they knew from school or heard about on TV. Others they became aware of at that moment who they were and what their story was. They began to interact with the people. They were introduced to Plato, Charlemagne, Sir Isaac Newton, Albert Einstein and many others. Mikaela especially liked meeting J.R.R Tolkien.

"Mr. Tolkien, I really enjoyed your books and movies," Mikaela said.

"Movies?" the great author questioned.

"Oh sorry, they were made after you...ah..."

"After I died?"

"Oops sorry."

"No need to be sorry my child. That is reality. We all pass and then go to live where we are supposed to live, here with the Great Light."

"I suppose you already knew your books were turned into movies. Being here you must know everything?"

The author shook his head with a smile. "No, once you are here there is no need to look back. No need to see what is happening on Earth."

The children continued to enjoy meetings with the people of the past. The other great thing about meeting these people was that they were not all famous. There were people who had been bus drivers, janitors, florists, bakers, and all of them were viewed as having the same value as those who had been famous on Earth.

As they continued their conversations they could see through a great window that darkness was setting on the horizon toward their home.

"Looks like the sun is setting?" Zachary asked.

"Yes, in your world the sun is setting so you better return home. The doorway to our world will close soon as the light fades."

Mikaela and Zachary looked at each other. They didn't want to go home.

"Children, you need to go home. You need to help your family, especially your mother and Jake."

"Why Jake?"

"Your brother is going through a lot right now and you will need to help him one day."

"Help him? He never wants to talk to us!" Mikaela exclaimed.

"Your brother is going through a lot of changes. He is changing from a boy to a man and it can be difficult. And your mother now needs you more than ever"

The children agreed. They had been so lost in their new paradise that they had even forgotten about their dear mother who was now suffering with cancer. As the smaller physical sun was setting back on Earth, the Great Light continued to beam down on the rest of ----------------------.

"Can't we just call this place heaven?" Zachary said to Elethira.

"You can, it really is just an earthly term. Its real name is indescribable."

"All of this is," Mikaela said with profound reverence.

"Mother Light, are we able to come back?"

"Yes my children. When the sun shines its light on the two ceiling windows in the late afternoon, you will be able to see the outline of the door. I want you to come back so I can teach you more."

The children were relieved that they could come back. The orbs or "angels" then grabbed the three and gently escorted them back to the "doorway." They flew with the children, grasping them under their arms. The children screamed with joy as they were zooming in and out of trees, valleys, lakes and rivers. They then slowed down and landed on a hill with a steep cliff. Beyond the ledge of the cliff was nothing but clouds.

"Go ahead children, walk into the clouds."

"Won't we fall?"

"Don't you trust us?" one of the orbs said with a bright smile.

The children slowly moved through the clouds and were immediately ushered into the attic of their house.

"Wow, can you believe that?" Mikaela said with a shout.

Greta smiled a knowing smile and Zachary was giggling and somewhat in a haze. They immediately walked down to the kitchen where they saw Jayne. Both Mikaela and Zachary ran to their mother and gave her the biggest hug she had ever received.

"Wow what's with all the emotion?"

"We just love you so much mama!" Zachary said with tears of joy in his eyes.

"Mom, everything is going to be okay," Mikaela said with an energy that was even greater than her normal exuberance.

"What were you kids doing up there? You must have had a great time to be so happy?"

"We just realized how much we love you mom!" the trio looked at each other deciding they probably shouldn't mention anything about their adventure.

Across town, Jake was with his friends at the "hideout." He felt that since he had been good for the past several weeks and his grades had improved, his parents wouldn't question his "staying after school to study" fable.

"Hey Jake, long time no see," Will Staton said as he handed him a joint.

"We thought you no longer wanted to be one of the Black Knights!" said Mac, looking completely intoxicated. Jake shrugged his shoulders.

"My folks have been making me work in the new house, it's a ton of work."

"C'mon man, you're almost seventeen. You still doing what your parents tell you?!!!"

"What else am I going to do?"

"Tell 'em to chuv it!"

Jake remained silent. The boys continued to take hits off a joint that was being passed around.

"I bet he's still a virgin," Mac began to snigger.

Jake smiled a confident smile.

"You're not a virgin?"

Jake shook his head."

"When did this happen?"

"About a week ago?"

"Who was it?"

"It's a girl from the Catholic high school."

"What's her name?"

"Stella."

"So what did you do?" Asked Mac incredulously.

"Well, she's a little older than me so she kind of, kind of…"

"Instructed you?" Breck said scoffing.

"Well, I mean clearly she was experienced so I did let her control things," Jake said hoping his lie sounded plausible.

Jake had the boy's full attention now, as if he had just manifested himself into a ghost.

"Then what happened?" a practically gasping Will Staton asked.

"She took my clothes off and then pushed me onto the cot."

"What cot?"

Jake thought for a moment. Should he divulge the secret hiding place of Stella?

"Sorry, I meant bed. It's Stella's bed. In her bedroom. At her house."

Jake was getting concerned that his story was sounding manufactured as of course it was. The boys ignored the fabrication and implored Jake for more details.

"She then took her clothes off and got on top of me. She began to kiss me and well…the rest is history."

"Man you dog!"

"That sounds similar to what happen to me with Katie Perkins," Mac said.

"You never got anywhere with Katie Perkins you liar!" Will Staton yelled, secretly wanting to be Katie's boyfriend.

For another hour the boys laughed and talked. Jake now had a new-found sense of importance and his stock had gone up considerably within the Black Knights.

Later that night Jake came home to find his mom crying at the kitchen table.

"Mom, what is it?"

"Nothing Jake. It's just this chemo that's making me sick.

"You're on chemo?"

"Yes, just started a few days ago. Where have you been? You smell funny."

"Oh it's just some cologne my friend Will gave me."

"Cologne. Why on Earth do you need cologne? You're not trying to cover up something are you?"

"No, it's just that I'm thinking about going to the junior prom this year and was taking some advice from Will about what to wear, that's all."

Jake could see that his mother was in a vulnerable and weakened state. Should he lie to his sainted mother like that? Yes, he did want to go to the junior prom, especially since he now had a girl in his life, but the real reason for the scent was to disguise that of another. He touched his mother on the arm. She looked up at him, looking into his eyes. She knew that her once innocent, darling son was no longer so innocent. He seemed to have a worldliness about him. He reached in and gave her a peck on the forehead, stroking her hair gently. Jayne was surprised. She had never received any sort of affection from Jake like that since he was very young. She gave him a faint smile and placed her hand on his.

"Good night mom."

As Jake walked upstairs to his room, he began to feel compassion for his mother. Yes, he wanted to be grown up, to be a man, but he didn't want his mother to suffer. Was she suffering because of him, because of all the stress he had placed on her the past couple of years? He didn't know. He closed the door behind him and pondered his relationship with his parents. That soon subsided however as his thoughts turned to Stella in the basement.

After his parents had gone to bed, Jake crept down to the kitchen where he made Stella a turkey sandwich. He poured her a tall glass of milk and then headed down to the basement. He knocked gently on the door and Stella soon appeared. She smiled and beckoned for him to come in. She quickly devoured the sandwich like she hadn't eaten in days. Her attention then turned to Jake.

"Hey Jakey, what is it? You look a little distracted."

"Oh, it's my mom. We just found out she has cancer."

"Oh Jake, I'm so sorry," she said as she hugged him. It was a long, warm hug and he welcomed it.

"What's her prognosis?"

"I'm not sure. They think they might have caught it in time but we're not sure…" his voice trailed off.

"Don't worry, everything will be fine."

"How do you know?"

"I just do."

Jake stared into her beautiful eyes. Whether it was true or not the confidence she evoked was encouraging. She began to message his neck and shoulders.

"There is that helping?"

"Yes, very much so."

"You know what might take your mind of your troubles?"

"What?" Jake said, wondering and hoping what her solution might be.

"I make a sketch you."

Jake's mind began to wonder. Did she want to sketch him in the nude? He noticed her looking at him in a rather odd way the last time they had met. She had asked him to stand and walk around while she eyed him like a piece of meat.

"Ah sure, how do you want me to pose?"

Stella thought for a while. A bright smile began to appear on her face. Was it what Jake was hoping for?

"How about you keep your clothes on and sit over here by the end of the cot?" she said with a coy wink that drove Jake crazy.

"I want you to lean back against the wall. Raise one leg up so you can rest your arm on your knee. Then lower you head on to your arm." Stella helped move and mold her living mound of clay exactly into the position she wanted. All the while Jake thoroughly enjoyed it.

"There! You are the living embodiment of *a somber soul* – that is the title of the sketch."

For the next thirty minutes, Jake sat motionless as Stella sketched his image. The result was quite amazing. Jake felt as though Stella captured not only the physical image but the pain and the emotion of his character.

"Wow, that's incredible. You are a great artist! You should be a professional!"

"I am."

"You are?"

"Yes, now pay me ten dollars," Stella demanded with a smile.

"Oh, ah sure," Jake said, taking out his wallet and giving her the remnant of his allowance. She walked over to him and gave him a long passionate kiss. His heart started pounding and he wasn't sure where this show of affection was leading to. He didn't care. She eventually relented and pulled back. Giving him a quick peck on the lips and walking back to the cot.

It took Jake a while to calm down from the encounter. When he did get in control of his senses, he turned to look at Stella. He couldn't believe he had such a beautiful girl living right in his own basement. He wanted to tell the whole world, but he couldn't. How would he get their relationship to the next level? A level where they could be seen socially? He wanted to take her to the junior prom.

"How much longer do you think you need to hide out?"

"I'm not sure."

"Aren't the police looking for you?"

"No. Before I ran away, I left a note on the refrigerator door. I told them that I was going to live with my boyfriend who happens to be the son of a sheriff down in Florida. I told them if they tried to find me I would tell my boyfriend's dad what they were doing to me."

"Do you mind if I ask what they were doing to you?"

"Emotional abuse…sometimes physical. My mom would call me a whore. I mean all I wanted to do was hang out with my friends and they thought I was running around prostituting myself."

Jake was quiet. He could see the pain on her face. It seemed like a simple request for her to spend time with her friends so he began to feel great sympathy for her.

"Well, why don't you start hanging out with me and my friends? We could go to the junior prom…"

"That's impossible. If my parents found out I was still in town it would be over."

"But are you going to stay in this basement forever?"

"I just need more time to think about what I'm going to do."

Jake rolled over on his side. Stella grabbed him by the shoulder and rolled him back over so he could face her. She smiled at him and began to stroke his chin. She then began to run her finger over his mouth.

"Just be patient with me," she said with an expression that made Jake melt. It was a look that gave Jake courage. He would fight the entire world if necessary to keep her safe.

CHAPTER 5

Search for a Cure

The entire family, with the exception of Jake waited in the lobby of the doctor's office. An assistant opened the door and asked them all to enter. She walked them into a large office that was surrounded with books; wall to wall. Behind a large desk was a small woman with long dark hair tied back. She was typing on her computer. She looked up to see the family.

"Hello Royaltons, please be seated."

Jayne, Charlie, Mikaela and Zachary all took seats that were in a half circle around the doctor's desk.

"Well we have some bad news and some good news."

Jayne nodded awaiting to hear the worst.

"The chemo is not having the effect we had hoped but I am in contact with a specialist in the stem cell field and immune therapy drugs who I think can help you."

"I wasn't on chemo for very long."

"Yes, but you are not reacting well to the treatments and it's not having much effect. You still have an extremely high white blood cell count."

Mikaela and Zachary looked on, somewhat confused by their own presence. They wanted to help their mother as much as they could and so they agreed to attend her doctor's visits with her. The doctor and Jayne had decided it was best not to hide anything from the children. Jake on the other hand was not dealing with it as well and had refused.

"There's an oncologist in Medford I would like you to visit. Her name is Dr. Zhang. I want you to visit her next week and see if what she can offer will help you, otherwise we'll need to get very aggressive with the chemo."

Jayne nodded her head while Charlie clasped her hands in his. Mikaela patted her mother on her arm trying to show support. Zachary stared off into space, dreaming of when he could visit heaven.

******

With his grades much improved and being around home more, Jake was rewarded by his parents with some newfound freedom and an increase in his weekly allowance of $25. He also got his cellphone back and the chance to use the SUV when it was available. He decided to take the $100 Old Navy gift card he was given by his grandmother and go on a little shopping spree with Stella. Apart from a couple of school uniforms the only other items she had kept in the basement were a t-shirt, sweatshirt, sweatpants and a pair of jeans. Along with her bedsheets, Jake had been washing her clothes late at night when his parents had gone to bed. It usually corresponded with their nightly trysts and snack time.

A little nervous about their venturing out, Stella felt pretty comfortable that her parents would never go to the Milltown Mall. Jake was also comfortable that the Black Knights would not be there either. The mall was on the complete opposite end of the city so they should be safe, they both thought.

After buying Stella a new pair of jeans and several tops from Old Navy, they decided to head to the food court, but before they did, Stella grabbed Jake by the arm and pulled him into the Victoria Secret store. Completely embarrassed Jake did not know what to do. Stella laughed at him as she showed him lacey bras and various types of lingerie. She eventually bought herself a black teddy that Jake was in complete agreement with.

"Aren't you two a little young for this?" the cashier asked as they checked out.

"Oh, this is for my mom," Stella said in the most confident voice she could muster. The cashier gave a look of suspicion as she continued to process a gift card Stella presented her. She then grabbed Jake by the hand and they ran over to the movie theatre where they bought tickets for the next show. They headed to the rear of the theatre where they could snuggle. Jake felt so mature. He had heard about what young couples did in the back of theatres. Stella rested her head on his shoulder and he put his arm tightly around her. *Could this be love?* he wondered to himself.

The movie was quite boring and so they decided to make out. They had not done much kissing previously, and so this was a somewhat new experience for Jake, one that he liked quite a bit. This new encounter made him feel even closer to Stella. They seemed to be connected on a higher level. They couldn't speak given the nearby crowd, nor would it matter since the volume was so high. But they felt like they were in their own, naughty little world. After a while they both pulled back locking foreheads and smiling brightly at each other. If this wasn't love then Jake had no clue what was. It was if they could read each other minds. Stella was telling Jake that she loved him and needed his protection; his protection from her parents, his protection from the world.

They continued to stare into each other's eyes. It was not the least bit difficult or even noticeable to them. It seemed like only minutes as they stared. They both had not realized that the movie had stopped and the show had ended over a half-hour earlier. It was suggested by the attendant that they should leave. They both burst into laughter when they realized what had happened.

Stella grabbed Jake's hand and led him out of the theatre. They drove back home and she led him down to the basement. Wanting to keep the intimacy going from their encounter in the theatre, Stella pushed Jake onto the cot and they began making out. As they continued kissing, they could hear the rest of the family arriving back home. This was the signal that Jake needed to hurry up and get back upstairs. He gave Stella a kiss goodbye and immediately bolted up to the kitchen.

"Jake, what a surprise to see you coming up from the basement, again," his dad said with a weary smile.

"Yeah, I found some old CDs I might like to listen to."

"Do we even have a CD player anymore? I thought you downloaded everything these days?"

"I'm kinda retro. I'm even thinking about buying a stereo.'

"A stereo? I haven't heard about those in years. Are they even making them anymore?"

"Yeah, they make 'em for DJs, you know for parties and stuff. How's mom?" he asked the question in a hushed tone.

"Not so good. Her spirits are down. Go give her a hug."

Jake smiled and did exactly that.

"Hi mom, how are you?"

"Better now that you're here. I need a hug."

Jake complied and gave her a strong, long hug. Despite everything that was happening to him he still loved his parents and especially his mother. Mikaela and Zachary were surprised to see their big brother so animated. They didn't realize that he had a new outlook on life. One that had been developing over the past couple of weeks.

******

The next day, Mikaela and Zachary began to play out in the field behind their house. They were hoping by playing there that Greta would see them and come join them. She hadn't been around for the past couple of days and that was unusual. As her father had said, "that trio is as thick as thieves." She wasn't sure what that meant but knew he was referring to how close the friends had become, and even closer after their encounter with the divine.

They settled into a flat grassy area of the field and then dropped a soccer ball to start kicking it around.

"Hey, wait for me!!!"

The siblings turned around and could see way off in the distance toward Greta's house a figure starting to appear through the woods. It was Greta. Both Mikaela and Zachary started to run in her direction while kicking the ball. They were all smiles and couldn't wait to meet their friend.

"Greta! Where have you been?!!!" Mikaela shouted. The trio met in the middle of the field and began to hug each other. They were practically screaming with delight. They had not seen each other since their trip to "heaven."

"So, where have you been hiding?"

"My dad had a business trip out of town and took me along."

"Where did you go?"

"I'm not sure exactly. We drove to a city out east, somewhere near Allentown. He had business there."

Not really caring what the reason was, Mikaela and Zachary grabbed Greta and the three walked arm-in-arm toward the Royalton's house. In the field by their house they played soccer and ran around until they were practically dizzy.

Finally exhausted they plopped themselves down into some high soft grass and took a breather. The sun was starting to get lower in the sky and they could see rays of light starting to beam down on the ceiling panels and windows.

"Well, are you guys ready for another adventure?"

"What do you mean?"

"See the way the sun is beaming down on those windows?"

"Yeah,"

"Well, that means the portal is about to open again."

"You mean that wasn't a dream we had?" Zachary asked with surprise.

"No, that really happened."

"Wow, how do you know about all this Greta?" Mikaela asked.

"She's an angel, remember Mickey?"

"You'll see. C'mon, let's go to the attic!"

Mikaela and Zachary could barely contain themselves. The three popped up in unison and started running for the house. They tore through the back door of the kitchen and then ran upstairs.

"Hey mom, we're gonna play up in the attic!" Mikaela yelled as they passed their mom in the kitchen.

As the three arrived in the attic, they could see a beam of light slowly pass through the middle of the room and eventually end up against the far wall. As it reached the wall they could see the door. They immediately rushed to the door, pulled up on the rope and pushed the door open. As before, there laid before them paradise. And like before they were overwhelmed with what they saw. Now they knew it had not been a dream. This was real.

"Whoa, I can't believe this place!" Zachary cried.

The three began to run into the field that was surrounded by clouds, soon basking in the rays of the Great Light as they ran and ran. They were soon flying and began to zoom through the trees and fields, swooping down through hills and gulleys, ravines and mountains. Zachary propelled himself over a river and placed his hand in the crystal waters causing a great spray of water to billow behind him. Greta and Mikaela laughed at his antics.

Soon the children arrived at the Great Temple and were met by Elethria, Lumina, Gallatam, Selebria and Niamthan.

"Hello children," said Elethria. "I see you've learned to fly."

Mikaela and Zachary thought for a moment. Didn't they fly the last time they were here? They realized that they had only been walking on their last visit. Had they learned a new skill without realizing it?

"I don't know Mistress," Mikaela put a finger to her chin and began to think. "All I know is that I was just flying, I wasn't even thinking about it."

"That's your inner-being growing. The light you have inside you is from the Great Light. The Great Light is teaching your inner-being on how to grow spiritually. As you grow spiritually you lose the bounds of the natural Earth and you become free."

"Wow, that's awesome!" Zachary exclaimed.

"Come children, Mother Light wishes to instruct you."

The children walked with the orbs toward the back of the temple where Mother Light was seated at the banquet table they had previously dined at.

"Children, please join me," Mother Light said and invited the children to partake in another feast. The children dined on the most wonderful and exotic fruits and vegetables. They then stuffed themselves with various pies and pastries, washing it down with the most delicious cider they had ever tasted. Once they were satisfied, Mother Light began to instruct them.

"Children, it is difficult for you to see now what the real world is. You live in a world that has been corrupted by mankind's greed and selfishness. Because humans do not have the full light they live in a type of darkness where they can only see things partially. You live in a state of development and your goal is to become a completely spiritual being. You want to become one with the Great Light."

As Mother Light spoke, the children felt waves of love and affection flow over them. They only knew the moment, a seemingly eternal moment; there was no time, no past no future. They didn't want to move. They just wanted to exist, exist in the warmth of the Great Light.

"What you see in your world are representations of what can be. You have a sun. That sun is vast and it revolves in a galaxy that is even more vast, but those things only pale in comparison to the Great Light. They are just mere representations of the Great Light. The home you live in, the fields behind your house that you play in are all just representations of something much greater."

"But why is the world we live in so…so…"

"Inferior?"

"Yes," Mikaela said, thankful that Mother Light could read her mind.

"Mankind has rejected the Great Light. Mankind and womankind have decided to follow their own path. That path is flawed and leads to confusion. Even the most basic things like why creatures were created male and female become confused in your world. Humans are so disoriented by their need to follow their own wills that they become blind. Yes, they can see things in the physical world, but they are completely blind to the spiritual world…the true world."

"How can we fix it?" Zachary asked.

"By seeking the Great Light. If you seek the Great Light, people will see that you are different. They will see that you are good and kind and they will want to have what you have; a real peace, real joy. That is why your mission on Earth is not complete. You need to show your friends and most importantly your mother and brother what the truth is."

"And what is that truth?"

"The truth is that there is something greater than the Earth. There is something much more to each human being. They have in them the potential to be incredible spiritual beings, if only they sacrifice their needs and desires for others. And it is your job to teach them that."

"But Mother, we are only kids."

"Yes you are, and what better way to communicate to others than that of innocent, untainted children. All you need to do is seek the Great Light. People will see the light inside of you and will ask how they can have the same thing."

"What do we tell them?"

"To give up their vices, give up their selfish desires and to help others."

"Is that it?"

"No, but it is a start."

The children began to look at each other with big smiles. They had no idea they had such an important mission to complete. And now it was time to go back home. They could see the light setting in the west, which as they learned was merely a reflection of their earthly world. But, it was time to go home. This time, instead of being escorted by the orbs, they simply flew back to the portal and entered right into the attic with no hesitation. The children looked at each and began to giggle, they had never experienced such joy before. They hugged and then ran downstairs to be with Jayne.

CHAPTER 6

A Bungled Burglary

Feeling a little depressed about his mother, Jake decided to hang out with the Black Knights. While his new relationship with Stella was something of great pride, he had a feeling of ennui. Most regular, red-blooded American boys would love having a beautiful girl living in their basements, but for some reason Jake was feeling there was something lacking in his life. He was learning that striving for sex, while a lot of fun, was not an answer for everything. Trying to satisfy his sexual needs was not going to cure his mother's cancer.

Over the past several meetings, Jake learned that Mac and Will were having major problems at home. Mac had an abusive father and Will's mother, a single parent, was seldom at home and was an alcoholic. She left little for Will at home in the way of food and other supplies. Jake did his best to encourage them but he could tell both boys were getting depressed and agitated. Their taste in drugs had also changed, preferring now to snort coke or heroin. For Jake the change was not good and he did his best to discourage the boys from taking harder drugs. The more they got depressed, the more relief they sought.

The increase in Mac and Will's drug use was starting to become a problem. These drugs were more expensive and they soon were running low on money. Jake and Breck, both wary of where Mac and Will's drug use was heading, were using less and less themselves; preferring only to take an occasional hit off a joint.

"Hey, I'm really in need of some cash," Mac said.

As Mac said this, Jake could see a bruise on his cheek. Clearly things were getting bad for Mac.

"Why do you need money?"

"To score some dope you dweeb!"

"Well, I don't have any," Will replied.

"I know you guys are broke but I know somewhere where we can get some."

"Where?"

"There's an elderly couple down the street from me. My family has known them for years. I used to cut the grass for them and would go inside their house from time to time. They have some really nice things in there. I'm sure we can score some jewelry and cash!"

"Look, I don't know about this Mac. What if we get caught?"

"C'mon you lily-livered bastard. We all need money. I need to get out of my dad's place. Will needs food, you've got that new girlfriend whom I'm sure needs some fancy things."

It was true. Jake's allowance was not going too far these days. Most of it he spent on hot meals at school and what little he had left over he would buy things for Stella.

"C'mon man, these people are rich. They're a bunch of snobs, always looking down on my family. They need to be brought down a bit. Let's go tonight. The Black Knights on a mission!!!"

The other three boys were not so sure. Will hadn't seen his mother in weeks. He had one box of macaroni and cheese left in the cupboard. He had finished consuming the last of the cheerios he had for breakfast. He was famished.

"Yeah, I'm starving. I really need some food."

"Yeah and I need a place to live," Mac said with sadness.

Jake began to feel for his friends. He looked at Breck who remained silent throughout. Breck had a relatively good life at home. He wasn't wealthy but his family had a solid middle-class income. He had been excelling at sports and was hoping for a scholarship to the University in a couple of years. He didn't want to mess that up.

"Hey guys, sorry, but I need to head home," Breck said, wanting to avoid any further involvement with the Black Knights.

"You coward! Now that it's come to a serious point, you just run away. You are not a loyal knight!"

"I may not be, but at least I'm staying out of jail!"

Before they knew it Breck was out of sight, having disappeared into the woods.

"What'ya say Jakey, you want to help us?"

Jake was silent. He could see the boys needed his help, but what would happen? What if they got caught? What if they accidently hurt one of the residents?

"Look, whatever we get I will split with you three ways. I'm sure we'll get a least a grand each."

Jake studied Will and could see he was looking gaunt. It looked like he hadn't eaten in a while. His face looked pale and he didn't look healthy at all.

"Do you think you should maybe go to a doctor Will?"

"How can I go to a doctor? I don't have any money."

"C'mon Jake, you got to help us."

Jake nodded and the boys made plans for later that night. In the meantime Jake went home to have dinner with his family. When he came home he found his siblings and father at the dinner table.

"Where's mom?"

"She's lying in bed upstairs. She's not feeling well."

"Aren't you guys going to see that specialist soon?"

"Yes, tomorrow. Did you want to come?"

"Maybe…I'll see. I've got a lot of homework."

Charlie nodded while Mikaela and Zachary eyed their brother up and down. They didn't know if he was understanding what was happening to their mother. The truth was he was trying the best he could to bury his feeling deep inside.

After dinner, Jake went upstairs to his room. He thought about Stella in the basement and planned to bring her some food before he left on the Black Knight's "mission." At 11pm he slipped down to the kitchen and put some leftover spaghetti into the microwave. He poured a glass of milk and then headed down to the basement. He rapped gently on the door and was soon admitted by Stella into the hideout. She quickly gobbled down the pasta while Jake looked around the room. He was convincing himself the robbery was a good idea so that he could start providing some furniture and other bric-a-brac to help brighten up an otherwise spartan room. Once she completed her meal she told Jake that she was tired and wanted to go to sleep. He gave her a kiss and then quickly exited.

****

Later that night, Jake met Will and Mac in front of Mac's house. Jake was starting to feel apprehensive and nervous. He wasn't quite sure why he was doing it. He felt compelled to help Will but he knew what he was doing was wrong. The three then walked to the backyard where there was a dried riverbed. It was a tributary that led for several miles back toward the marsh behind Arendelle Court. They walked through the riverbed for a quarter of a mile until they came upon the house that was the target.

"Okay, this is it. We just need to climb over the fence and then pry one of the windows open. I've got a crowbar."

Mac had a large sack which Jake assumed was where the loot would be placed. It was also where Mac had concealed the crowbar and what looked like rope.

"Tell me no one is going to get hurt right Mac?" Jake asked with a pleading voice.

"Just settle down. No one will get hurt."

"What's the rope for?"

"In case we have to restrain anyone. I also have duct tape if needed."

"Let's just get this over with. If anyone stirs then we just need to leave, understood?"

"Fine. Here's your masks," Mac pulled out three black ski masks. Will and Jake quickly pulled them over their heads. Mac scaled the wood fence with Jake and Will in close pursuit. The backyard was large and well-manicured. There were plenty of bushes and trees to hide behind as they made their way to the house. Thankfully there were no lights on as they stepped onto the back porch. Mac looked through the back windows and confirmed no one was around. He took the crowbar and gently wedged it into the door jam. He pushed slightly but then the creaking and splitting of wood started to make too much noise.

"I don't think that's going to work Mac."

Mac then grabbed a rag from the duffel bag and began to wrap it around the crowbar. He then punched a hole through one of the windows of the backdoor. They waited quietly to make sure they hadn't awoken anyone. He then put his hand through the broken glass and then undid the lock. He turned the knob and they were in. Mac had a small flashlight which he pointed around as they walked through the kitchen and the dining room.

"Here, I have a bag for each of you. Take whatever looks valuable," Mac said in a whisper. The boys stepped lightly through the dining room looking for any valuables. So far they had not encountered anything and surmised that anything like jewelry would be in the couple's bedroom. They began to walk down the hallway that led to the master bedroom. It was an older home and each time the floor panels creaked the boys had to stop. As they moved down the hall, Mac pointed to Jake to go in one of the other bedrooms. Jake complied and began to look around. There was a full moon and with no curtain on the window, he could see the contents of the room clearly. He saw a desk that looked like it was being used to do bookkeeping. There was a floor safe but that didn't do him any good unless he was good at safecracking which he was not. He looked through the drawers of the desk and found several items of interest; a gold watch, some cufflinks and a writing pen set that appeared to be gold. He quickly placed those into his sack.

As Jake walked over to the closet, he could hear some commotion down the hallway. He walked to the doorway and could see Mac and Will running toward him.

"Get out of here!!!" Mac yelled.

Behind the boys was a man who had a shotgun in his hands. He was older but was making a steady pace. Jake turned and began to run as fast as he could toward the kitchen.

"I'll get you bastards!!!" the man screamed.

Mac, Jake and Will ran faster than they had ever done before. They pushed the kitchen door open, jumped off the landing and stairway onto the back patio and ran toward the fence. Mac and Will were up and over the fence while Jake started to climb. He looked back and could see the old man about to take aim with his shotgun. He fired the gun and Jake could hear a bullet whiz by his head and splinter a nearby tree. The force of the shot knocked the old man against the back door where he seemed to have passed out. Jake quickly climbed over the fence, dropping his bag of loot in the backyard as he did so. The boys began to run back toward Mac's house.

Once at Mac's house, Mac headed toward his bedroom window to sneak back in. Will and Jake continued running through the riverbed back to their homes. Jake patted Will on his back when they arrived at Will's house. Jake gave Will a look of concern and then looked back toward the Harris home. They could hear dogs howling throughout the neighborhood. The two boys were silent, not knowing what had happened to the old man. They imagined that the police would arrive soon. Jake waved to Will and then continued to run down the riverbed until he came to the end of the neighborhood. He then ran down the dark streets until he finally arrived at Arendelle Court. He had never been happier to be home. He immediately went upstairs to his room, closed the door and plopped down in bed. He prayed for forgiveness and then went to sleep.

CHAPTER 7

Lessons from Paradise

After school the children met in the attic again and waited for the sunlight to hit the wall in just the right angle. As it did, the door became visible. They quickly unlatched the door and ran into the open field. Like jet aircraft they slowly lifted into the air and were flying higher and faster than they did before. They were learning more and more about flying each time they entered heaven. During their second trip they had awkwardly learned that they could bounce around and soon find themselves weightless. Toward the end of that visit they knew they could fly and did so. Now they were zooming around like the orbs they had first met.

The experience of flying through high cumulus clouds and to seeing an endless horizon filled the children with such exhilaration, like nothing they had ever experienced. They could see oceans and mountains larger and much more vibrant than back on Earth. They started to realize that everything was much more vibrant because they could see much more. It was like looking at a computer screen that had a finite number of pixels per square inch, but now having entered this new world, that screen had an infinite number. It was like seeing something the size of an atom and then being able to see the universe. The Great Light revealed not only physical images but spiritual images. With each visit to heaven they were seeing so much more. It was like they no longer had physical eyes, they could see in a 360-degree vision. While at first breath-taking it was soon just second nature to them.

After zooming far and wide, they knew that Mother Light was calling them and they quickly returned to the Temple. This time there was no food. There was no need as they realized they were being filled spiritually and did not need physical food.

"Children, we have a long lesson today so I would like to get started. Please take your seats at the table and concentrate on what I have to say."

The children did not really need to concentrate. They feasted on every word Mother Light spoke. It was as if with each word they felt a great love swarm all around them. They wanted more and more and more. They were in complete bliss as their mother continued to speak.

"Children, as you have been going back and forth between your world and this, you are starting to understand the differences between light and dark. When things are illuminated you can see and understand. But back in your world, people are wandering around in darkness. And when they stumble around they make grave errors. Those errors cause even more darkness and it becomes a darkness that people eventually cannot escape from. It will be your job to help people to see the light."

"But Mother Light, how can we do that? We are only a couple of kids."

"Do not say that. You are children of the light and no one can take that away from you. You have been selected to be here. Like Greta you have love in your hearts and you want to learn and to do good, therefore you have been permitted to see heaven. Don't worry about things my little lights. You will grow in stature and wisdom and you will be respected. People will listen to your words."

Mikaela was not entirely convinced but she knew that Mother Light knew all.

"One area that the world has really become dark on is the role of human beings. Each human being was born male and female. This is a special creation from the Great Light. It allows people to interact in a beautiful way."

"But people are telling us in school that there are no genders anymore – that it was just an old way of labeling people."

"Do you believe that?"

Mikaela thought for a moment.

"I don't know. Sometimes I feel boys have special advantages that girls do not have. It seems unfair sometimes."

"It is true that sometimes there is inequality. But because there are times when things are not right, it doesn't mean that you throw away that thing. You see children, the differences between male and female are spiritual. Girls grow into women and women become mothers and being a mother is the greatest thing that one can attain."

"Really? I hear a lot of women, like my mom say that the most important thing for girls is to have a career."

"It can be important. There have been great women who have accomplished great things in science, politics, medicine…but it's not the greatest thing to be. There is nothing more important than having children, nurturing them and then educating them. No other job is more important."

"But why do women have to be stuck with that job?"

"You are not looking at that job in the correct light."

As Mother Light spoke, clarity of mind came to Mikaela and she could see what the true nature of being female was.

"The world makes those things in life that are important not so important. That is because the world casts a shadow over the good things. The good things are light and the darkness will overshadow it if it can."

"So I can't be an astronaut or pilot or professional soccer player?"

"Of course you can, but those things are not nearly as important as being a mother. Women can certainly choose, but if they try to be both it will be difficult. It will affect their lives tremendously if they do not choose one over the other. If they try to do both they will be trying to split themselves in half. It is better to do one over the other."

"Sometimes I wonder about my mother and her decisions."

"Yes. Unfortunately your mother's decision to do both has made her sick. It has been too much of a strain on her. She loves her career and she loves you and Zachary and Jake but it has weakened her."

"Is that because women are weak?"

"No, not at all. Men are the weaker sex. Women get to be mothers and as a mother you learn what is most important. Men do not have that advantage."

"But why do men and women do things separately like in sports?" Zachary asked.

"Men can be physically stronger than women that is true but that is more a function of being a protector and provider of the family when mankind was first created."

"When was mankind created?"

"A long, long time ago. The seeds of human life were planted billions of Earth years ago, which is only a short time for those of us in heaven."

The children were amazed at what they were hearing and wanted to know more.

"But going back to being mothers…how is that more important than say a scientist who finds a cure for cancer?"

"Giving life is the most important thing. Look who you are talking to. I give life. I shine light on the world and life comes into being. Human beings need to come to the light, then there will be no need to fight cancer or to fight crime or abuse or anything dark. People do bad things and there are bad things in the world because people cannot see. They need the light."

Mikaela started to feel pride well up inside of her. She knew what Mother Light was saying was true. The most important thing for a woman was to become a mother and now she looked forward to that day when she would have children of her own. She used to dream about being the greatest female athlete of all time but now she knew there was something more to life than that.

"Now Zachary, you also have an important job. Your job is to become a great father and teach your sons how to be great fathers. Fathers need to love and take care of their wives. They need to feed and take care of the family, provide food and shelter and spiritual blessings as well. You also have an important job."

Zachary began to smile. He also liked the idea of having children one day.

"But I'm only eight."

"You are," Mother Light smiled with a most caring smile. "But one day you will be a young man and you will meet a young woman. You will fall in love and you will have a family."

"Can I be a soccer player first?"

"If you want to. You will settle on a career one day, but you will long to be with your wife and children. A career is only something that upholds the family, it is not anything that anyone should spend their whole lives pursuing. Educate yourself, go to school and learn a skill, trade, etc. But know that it is only a means to an end and your family is most important thing. The time you spend with your children is the most important job as well as supporting your wife."

The children nodded their heads but while they did so began to think of the negative comments they would receive back on Earth when they told people about this belief.

"Children, do not be worried about what to say to your friends and family, I will be helping you and giving you the words to say."

The children smiled feeling so much love in their hearts. They knew that they could only tell the truth and were excited to do so.

Mother Light smiled at them and told them it was time to leave. They immediately lifted from their seats into the air and began to fly back home. They were experiencing so much joy as they flew in tandem toward their home. As they approached the house they had an idea. They headed straight for the door and rather than opening it they just flew right through it. They tumbled into the attic and landed in a heap on top of each other. They burst into laughter at what had happened. They looked up at the ceiling windows and could see the sun just beginning to move out of sight. They looked at the door and could see that it was starting to fade.

"I wonder what would happen if we stayed too long in heaven?"

"I guess we would be stuck there."

"That would be a great place to be stuck!"

******

Jake walked into the school not wanting to be noticed. As far as popularity, Jake had always been an outsider trying to fit in. His efforts to assimilate varied depending on his mood and as of late, having a new girlfriend, albeit in the basement of his new home, he was less needy in that area. Still if the lead jock, or the head stoner, or the "person-most-likely-to-succeed" acknowledged his existence, he was downright honored and made life feel like it mattered. Today however he did not want to be acknowledged by anyone. He preferred to be anonymous. He headed into the door toward the back of the school which had the least amount of people. He quickly found his locker and placed his books inside, with the exception of his biology book that he needed for his first class.

Just as he closed his locker he was greeted by Will.

"Jake, did you hear what happened?"

"No."

"That old man that took a shot at us had a heart-attack and died."

"No, you're kidding!"

"Quiet!"

The two boys looked around realizing that Jake had made too much noise.

"What the hell do we do?" Jake said in an almost inaudible whisper.

"I don't know, but if they find out we were the ones that broke into the house they'll throw us in jail."

Will noticed the principal of the school walking down the hall. He shook his head and then began to walk in the opposite direction, hugging the wall as if hiding from the principal.

"Good morning Mr. Royalton."

"Good morning Principal Ramos."

Jake drew a sigh of relief as the principal continued down the hall. Jake then hightailed it over to his biology class. He passed Mac who was seated in the front row. He had his head in his arms as if asleep. As Jake passed him, one of Mac's hands reached out with a piece of paper. Jake grabbed it from his hand and continued to walk to his desk in the backrow.

Meet me at basecamp after school

Jake's mind began to race as he sat at his desk. He put his book on the desk and turned to the page that he knew they would be studying. At that point he seemed to be in another world; a dark and confused one. He felt like a zombie. The teacher came in and began to talk and as much as he tried to concentrate he could not understand what she was saying. It was as if she was speaking in another language. He continued in his daze until his lab partner Mark starting speaking to him and motioned for him to join him over in the lab. They were dissecting frogs that day. He went through the entire process feeling numb. He helped Mark make the necessary incisions and together they examined the insides of the frog but Jake was feeling like he was having an out-of-body experience. Like the dead frog, he could only think about the old man who was probably stiff and gray like the carcass he was looking at. He immediately ran to the bathroom and threw-up.

Across town at Roosevelt Elementary, the 4th graders were getting out for lunch. Mikaela was in her usual happy mood when she joined her "gang of girls" at the table. Along with Mikaela, Brittany Ryan was thought of as one of the leaders of the group. It was Mikaela and Brittany who usually made the decisions; especially as it related to sports during recess. The girls would divide into two teams; one led by Mikaela and one led by Brittany. In class it was always the same two girls who would raise their hands to answer questions. They would also be the first two to volunteer for any projects Mrs. Hanson their teacher handed out.

To say it was a fierce competition was an understatement.

"Hey, did you guys see the hat-trick Audrey Miller scored last night against Argentina?!!!" Becky Simmons said, looking for approval from the two alpha-females.

"Yeah that was awesome!" one of the more timid followers Marni Robins chimed in.

"Yeah, it was good, but not nearly as impressive as Sally Maycroft's five goals against Poland!" Brittany said with authority.

"C'mon, the women's national team of Poland is not nearly as good as the women's team from Argentina, right Mikaela?"

"Why are you guys so obsessed with soccer? It's not that important," Mikaela said, winking at Greta. The rest of the girls looked at Mikaela in astonishment. Mikaela was one of the top soccer players in the county. She had won a State Championship with her U9 team and was selected for a tryout at the girl's national regional.

"Look, you guys need to stop getting all geared up for this stuff. It's all going to go away some day. You need to focus on what is important. We girls get to be mothers one day!"

The girls continued to look at Mikaela like she had been supplanted by an alien.

"You've got to be kidding me!" Brittany said. "How can you say that? That's ridiculous.

One, we are too young to be mothers and two, who wants to be a mother when you can be a professional soccer player, or a doctor or an astronaut.”

“That’s the world talking Brittany. The world has lost all focus on priorities. Family is the most important thing.”

“So women are supposed to give up their careers and just become mothers?” Lola Sanchez said in a frail voice.

“No, we can be whatever we want to be. I’m just saying it’s more important to be a mother.”

“Where is this all coming from? Is it your dad telling you all this?”

“No, I’ve been spending time with a wise lady.”

“Who your mom? Your mom is one of the most professional women I know. She is one of the top professors at the university.”

“Yeah, well she might be paying for that.”

“What do you mean?”

“My mother has cancer.”

The girls all become quiet and sullen. They had no idea that Mikaela’s mother was sick. Mikaela had been the same happy-go-luck kid she had always been so the news that her mother was ill came as a great surprise and shock.

"Mickey, I'm sorry to hear that," Brittany said in a subdued voice. "I can understand why you are so anti-soccer right now."

"Because my mom is not doing well doesn't change my belief. I still think the most important thing we can do as girls is become good women and eventually mothers. Sports and careers are good, but they are not that important."

"So we just let boys have all the fun?"

"No, boys have a role of growing up and becoming great dads, that is what is most important for boys."

"Wow, this sounds all too grown-up for me," Lola said.

"This is crazy talk Mickey. You sound like one of those weird women on the black and white TV shows where they stayed home and just cleaned the house all day. You want to be like that?"

Mikaela sat and thought about it. She noticed a beam of light starting to hit the back wall of the cafeteria. She started to smile as a wonderful thought entered her head.

"It's not that being a housewife is important, it is being a mother that is important. Having children, taking care of them, nurturing them and educating them. It's the most important thing."

"Well for you maybe, but for me, I'm going to become a soccer player. No boy is going to tell me what to do."

"Why do you think some guy is going to tell you what to do?"

"Because that's how it went in the old days. Women were supposed to stay home; cook, clean, take care of the kids and do whatever their husbands told them to do because they were the 'bread-winners' or whatever they called them."

"Well, that's exactly why it's important to become a mom. When you have boys then you need to instruct them on how they are to treat women."

"You're getting really weird Mickey. I think you need to start playing soccer again to get your head right."

"Are girls in Germany taught to be just good housewives Greta?"

"No, but they should. Germany used to be a great country, but now people are just living for themselves. They just want to have great careers and they believe that they should spend their time either going to bars or being activists for every kind of group you can imagine."

"Like LGBTQ?"

"I mean anything. They either spend time going to school, drinking in bars or causing havoc by protesting about something. They have no purpose, nothing to live for. It's just darkness."

"What does your mom do?"

"She's no longer alive. She died when I was four."

"Really, how did she die?" Mikaela said in an apologetic tone. She never had asked about her mother before. She seemed to be very secretive of her parents. And given her "angelic" status she had stopped thinking of Greta in terms of being human.

"Cancer. Same as your mom," Greta looked deep in Mikaela's eyes as if speaking to her through extra-sensory perception, telling her that her mother would be okay.

At basecamp, Will, Mac and Jake assembled.

"What are we going to do?" Will said trembling.

"We're not going to do anything."

"We need to go to the police," Jake said in a raised voice.

"Keep it down. Look, if we go to the police and they find out why we were there…this is murder man. We're going to prison for a long, long time."

"Better that than going through life with this guilty conscience."

"Do you know what they do to people in prison? If you manage to stay alive from the constant beatings, then you get raped by gangs."

Jake and Will began to think about what prison was really like. Was that the truth or was it just from some movie that Mac had watched?

"Listen guys, we have to stay in unison on this. I'm not going to prison and if my dad finds out I won't even make it that far. He will literally kill me. I beg you not to go to the police."

Will looked like he was about to vomit. Jake's mind was racing and wasn't sure what he should do. For the moment he agreed to keep quiet.

"Look, that guy was eighty something anyway, he was about to die. He probably would have had a heart attack anyway."

While Mac's last comment somewhat eased Jake's mind, deep down he still knew it was wrong. At that point Mac lit a joint and the trio partook. They all needed relief from the stress. While they sat in a semi-circle taking hits from the joint, not a word was spoken. There was not the usual communal joking and postulating about universal truths. They had transgressed the law and that was enough to dwell on. Once they had finished the joint the three slipped into the dark forest in separate directions.

CHAPTER 8

Becky's Plight

As Mikaela and Zachary walked home from school, they noticed Becky Simmons sitting alone on a swing in the park near their home. The siblings walked over to her.

"Hey Becky! Are you doing alright?"

As Mikaela got closer to her she could see that Becky had been crying.

"What's wrong Becky?"

"It's my dad," she said, looking far into the horizon.

"What's the matter with your dad?"

"He just lost his job. They're cutting back at the plant and now he's out of work."

"I'm sure he'll find another job somewhere," Mikaela said, placing her hand on Becky's shoulder.

"I don't know, he's been really upset. He's says something about the economy and there are no mid-management jobs available. He says we might have to move."

"C'mon, come home with us. We'll get some cookies and we'll talk about it."

Becky smiled and agreed. She picked-up her backpack and headed to the Royalton home. As they arrived they greeted Jake who was arriving from the opposite direction. Jake grunted and quickly ran into the house.

Mikaela and Zachary led Becky into their kitchen. Mikaela called out to her mother but didn't receive a response. She told Becky to follow her and Zachary upstairs. They walked into their mother's room where they saw here lying in bed on her side.

"Mom, are you okay?" Mikaela asked.

Her mother turned over and raised herself up against her pillow.

"Yes dear, just resting," she said as she wiped her eyes.

"Is it okay if Becky stays for a while? We were going to have cookies and then hang out in the attic. Is that okay?"

"Sure dear. Boy, you sure are spending a lot of time up there. Must be fun."

Jayne then turned back onto her side trying to find a comfortable spot. Mikaela walked over to her and helped prop up her pillows.

"Thank you dear. You kids go have fun now."

Mikaela gave her a big hug. She could tell her mother was getting weaker and weaker. Zachary was somewhat oblivious to the situation. While aware that something was happening to his mother, he preferred not to think about it too much and when he did, he just hoped that the Great Light would heal her.

After cookies and milk, the three children made their way upstairs to play. Mikaela showed Becky around and they began to play with the castle their father had recently built for them out of wood. Zachary dressed up like a knight and pretended to fight a dragon while the girls hid in the castle. It wasn't so much hiding as it was having a little girl talk while playing with some dolls.

"Don't worry Becky. I'll talk to my dad. I bet he can find your dad a job."

"I hope so. I've never seen my dad so depressed. Normally he's happy and loves to spend time with us but lately he's really grumpy and just yells at us all the time."

Mikaela put her hand on Becky's shoulder.

"Look, these things happen. Don't worry, things will change."

As Mikaela said that she could see sunlight moving toward the back wall of the attic and as it continued to beam the portal became visible.

"Say, I have a great way to cheer you up. Let's go to a magical place."

"What magical place?" Becky asked incredulously.

"C'mon, I'll show you."

Mikaela and Zachary moved to the portal and pulled on the rope. Becky stepped forward and could see a bright beam of light coming through the door.

"How did a door get there?" she asked in a state of shock.

"It's a portal. A portal to heaven!" Zachary said excitedly.

"You're kidding," Becky said, transfixed like a zombie. She walked slowly toward the light not believing it could be true.

"C'mon, let's go!"

Mikaela and Zachary grabbed a hesitant Becky by the arms and then pulled her through the door.

"We're gonna fall!!!" Becky screamed with her eyes closed.

"No you're not silly. C'mon open your eyes."

Becky slowly opened her eyes and could see the vast gold and green field in front of her. There was a mist that she walked through and soon she began to chase after Mikaela and Zachary who were already sprinting.

"You ready to fly Becky?" Mikaela said as she and Zachary began to lift off.

"Wait, what are you doing?"

"Were flying, c'mon. Hurry up and join us!"

"But I can't."

"Yes, you can, you just have to believe you can."

Becky stared at Mikaela and Zachary who were zooming around and then eventually hovering over her.

"What is this place?"

"It's heaven."

"Heaven is a real place?"

"Yes it is, now let's get going. Start running fast and then leap into the air."

Becky began to run. She was in a sprint and then jumped as high as she could. She hit the ground but kept running and jumping. With each jump she could feel herself lifting off the ground further and further.

"Hey, I am flying!" She burst out into laughter enjoying the freeing sensation of flight.

"C'mon, we're gonna go to the Temple of Light."

"Temple of Light, what's that?"

"You'll see."

Mikaela and Zachary grabbed her by the arms and the trio zoomed through the air, weaving in and of trees and bushes, ravines and valleys. Becky screamed with delight the entire time. Soon they arrived at the temple and landed just outside of its gate. Inside were the orbs, waiting for the children with another feast. The children seated themselves and dug in. Becky couldn't remember the last time when she had had such a delicious meal. When they had finished, Mikaela pointed to Mother Light who had been waiting for them to finish.

"Mother Light, this is Becky."

"Yes, I know. Hello Becky, how are you?'

"I'm great, now that I'm here."

"Yes, but things are not going too well for you back on Earth."

Becky who had been in a complete state of euphoria suddenly came rocketing back to reality.

"Yeah, my dad's not doing too good."

"Too well."

"Oh, yes, too well." When Becky said this she perceived that she was speaking in a different language. It wasn't English, it was something else, something indescribable. But she understood everything that was being said. The sounds uttered by Mother Light were like music to her ears.

"Becky, do not be too disheartened. Your father is feeling the darkness. He is far away from the light right now, but you can help him see the light."

"But he gets so angry. Sometimes I think he will hit me or my mother or my sisters."

"He just needs a little help. You're a smart girl, you can help him."

"Yes, but how? I don't know anything about what he does. He's a manager or something, I guess."

"Maybe Mikaela can help. Can you help Becky's dad Mikaela?"

Mikaela thought for a moment and a smile soon grew on her face.

"Yes, yes Mother. I think I know what to do!"

"Excellent! You are all such smart children and you can figure out these things."

"Thank you Mother Light, I know what to do."

At that point, Mikaela grabbed Becky by the arm and motioned to Zachary to follow them. They ran into the sky and were soon airborne. They arrived back at the house within seconds and flew right through the portal and landed on their feet this time. They had truly gotten the knack of flying.

"C'mon, I've got an idea."

The three ran downstairs into the kitchen where they found Charlie making a sandwich.

"Hey dad, I need to talk with you."

"Yes, honey. What is it?"

"Can you get Becky's dad a job?"

"Well, I'm not sure. What does your dad do Becky?"

"He's a manager. I think it's something to do with computers."

"Well, we do have a pretty large IT department where I work. Do you know anything else about his job?"

Becky began to think about what he had said about his job in the past. She remembered him bringing home some drawings. The drawings looked like sketches of tubes or vents. She remembered once that he was working with some sort of computer program that looked at things in 3D.

"I think I heard him say something about designing vents. Stuff for houses and buildings."

"Hmmm, sounds like he works with CAD. I'll check around at work and see if we're hiring. My company is an engineering and design company so we might be able to help him. Can you give me your father's number?"

Becky smiled brightly and Mikaela handed her a piece of paper and pen to jot down her dad's number. Mikaela prayed that her dad could help Becky. Mikaela and Zachary then walked Becky home. As Becky went through the front door, she turned and smiled and waved to her friends.

"See you tomorrow Becky!"

Down in the basement, Jake was seeking solace from Stella. When he went down to her room she wasn't there. He knew she was spending more time away from the house but hoped it wouldn't be too long. He stood peering around the room and looked at her cot. He noticed a duffle bag he had not seen before lying on the floor next to her bed. He looked inside and found various pieces of clothing and underwear. He found a bra which was black and lacey. He imagined her wearing it and he immediately became aroused. He continued to rummage around in the duffel bag and found a magazine and some envelopes. The magazine was a teen fashion periodical he hadn't seen before. In the envelopes were various pieces of paper. Some of it looked like correspondence and others looked like crazy random thoughts or poetry:

Sometimes I feel like a pawn in a never-ending game

I feel used and defeated and sometimes ashamed

Never satisfied and frequently cry

Never happy I sometimes want to die

The night is cold and dark and I feel alone

Even when the day is bright I just want to groan

Never do I

The poem seemed to stop mid-thought. Jake became concerned about Stella's mental well-being. Given her circumstances he couldn't blame her. As he continued to read the next letter he noticed it seemed cryptic and really couldn't decipher its meaning:

> At house.
> Keeping watch.
> Making friends.
> Late night meetings.
> Establish ties.
> Daily parental activities.
> Food schedule.

Before he could read more, someone grabbed his arm and forced it behind his back. He tried to cry out but a hand clamped down over his mouth.

"What are you doing with my things Jake?"

Jake's arm began to hurt. He tried to speak but she kept her hand over his mouth.

"Look, just because I give you certain liberties you have no business going through my things. Do you understand?"

Jake nodded and then she let go. Jake turned to apologize. When he did so he noticed she looked a little more disheveled than normal.

"I'm sorry, I shouldn't have done that. It's just that I am going through a lot of things right now."

"I understand, but you have no right going through my things."

Jake nodded in agreement. Stella, sensing Jake's vulnerable state, pulled him toward her and she planted a long passionate kiss on his lips.

"Dos that make you feel any better?"

Jake nodded and smiled.

"How's your mom doing?"

"Not too good. She's been going to chemo and the doctor now wants her to try some other treatment I think."

"Boy, some son. You don't know what's happening with your mom."

"I'm having a hard time dealing with it. I don't like seeing her this way. It's making me crazy. And then on top of it I really did do something crazy."

"What was that?"

"I think I might have killed someone."

"Oh yeah, I heard."

"You heard?"

"You're talking about old man Harris right?"

"Yes, how did you know?"

"Oh, the news travels fast around here."

Jake began to think about the event and how it would be difficult to know about it.

"Why do you think you killed him?"

"Well, I…"

"Yes?"

"Well, I did something stupid. I helped Mac and Will rob his house, or at least we attempted to rob his house. He found us inside and then chased us. Before I got over the fence I could see him raise his shotgun. He fired and then fell over." Tears began to fill Jakes eyes. "It's because of us…me that he died."

"Don't worry about it sweetie. He would probably have died anyway. He was old."

Jake looked into Stella's eyes. Her comment seemed very cold and heartless.

"C'mon, you just need to forget about it."

As Stella grabbed him he motioned to her to wait. She tried to kiss him but he moved his head.

"What's the matter?"

"I feel really bad about Mr. Harris."

"C'mon, he was very old. Don't beat yourself up over it."

"God, if my parents knew about this they would kill me. I'm thinking I need to give myself up to the police."

"Don't be an idiot. Why go to jail over this?"

"It just seems like the right thing to do."

"It's not the right thing to do."

"Didn't your parents teach you to be honest?"

"My parents taught me nothing besides the fact that they were abusers."

"How did they abuse you?"

"Emotionally, verbally, physically."

"Your dad didn't do anything sexual did he?"

"No. But I wouldn't put it passed him. He was a fucking prick!"

Jake thought for a moment. He began to think about the idea of how a young girl could completely disappear from society and escape to someone's basement. He had read stories about how kids routinely disappeared. He remembered going to Walmart where near the bathrooms they posted pictures of missing and exploited children and teens. He wondered if Stella's pictured had been put up.

"What part of town are you from?"

"Um, ah Placerville."

"You mean Pacerville?"

"Um yea, sorry, had a brain fart there."

Jake began to grow suspicious of Stella.

"Where does your dad work?'

"Um, there's a factory there. He's like a manager."

Jake knew the Pacerville area very well. His soccer team often played there. It was very rural and mostly residential. There was no factory there. There was something wrong, but he put on a straight face so as not to arouse her suspicion that he knew something was up. He noticed that she was very strong and he didn't want to get on her bad side. He was starting to fear who he had gone in league with.

"Hey, I better get back upstairs."

As he got up from the cot, she grabbed him by the wrist. Her grip was strong. For an older teenage girl she seemed much stronger than the average teenage girl. She pulled him to her and looked into his eyes. She put her index finger to his lips.

"Remember you need to keep our little secret."

Jake nodded. He then quickly ran upstairs. Jake was feeling like his world was unravelling and had no idea what to do.

****

The next morning Jake joined the family for breakfast and then for the trip across town to be with his mother while she went through the new experimental treatment. The family filed out of the SUV in silence and all of them formed a bubble around their mother as they escorted her into the clinic. She was greeted by a nurse who described to her and the family what the procedure would entail. Jake was numb and was there in body only. His mind was racing and he felt like he would pass out at any moment.

After signing his wife in and given his insurance information, Charlie watched while another nurse greeted Jayne and was getting ready to escort her down the hall. The children rushed to their mother and gave her hug. Jayne pulled back and smiled.

"I will be alright. I love you."

The children buried their heads in her arms. Mikaela started to tremble, not knowing what was going to happen to her mother. Jayne brushed the hair out of Mikaela's eyes.

"It will be okay Mickey."

Mikaela started to feel a warm glow around her as her mother smiled. She hadn't had that feeling since the last time she had visited heaven.

Jake moved in closer and tears began to fill his eyes.

"It's okay Jakey. I love you." She cupped his chin in her hand and gave him a reassuring smile. The nurse motioned for Jayne to go with her and they were soon through the swinging doors and gone. The three children drew a breath of air. Mikaela and Zachary were happy, they knew their mother would be okay. They turned and looked at Jake who was trembling. They put their arms around him and Mikaela and gave him a bright smile.

"How can you guys be so calm?" he asked, as his voice slightly trembled.

"Mom will be okay. She will," Mikaela began to rub his arm. Jake looked at Mikaela. He had only seen her as his kid sister but now she had a calmness, a serene look of someone much older. He began to feel her confidence. Zachary also began to pat him on the back. It was the first time in their lives that the three had felt a connection. Throughout their lives, Jake had been the older brother and had never wanted to interact with his younger siblings. He had viewed them as annoying and taking attention away from him – his parents always fawning over them. The three walked over to several couches that were situated by a large screen TV. Mikaela and Zachary wanted to watch cartoons and given his newfound appreciation for his brother and sister he gave in to their request.

"You okay Jakey?" Jake's dad asked as he sat next to him on one of the couches. Jake nodded and looked ahead.

"Your mom's strong. She'll get through it," he said as he patted him on the knee. The four sat in the waiting room for three hours. Jayne emerged from the surgery room looking bright and cheerful. She was accompanied by her doctor. Dr. Chan sat with the family and went over what the procedure had entailed and cautioned against being too optimistic. Her mother would need to come back for further treatments but her hope was there should be improvement in her white blood cell count soon. Charlie thanked the doctor and they were soon headed home. They stopped at MacDonald's for dinner. Jayne tired quickly and so they wrapped up their trip to the Golden Arches prematurely.

As they made their way through the hills near their house the sun started to set. It seemed to become dark sooner than normal and Charlie was having issues negotiating the roads. The thick forest was blocking the sunlight. As he turned a corner too quickly, the car smashed into a deer. Charlie brought the car to a screeching halt and pulled to the side of the road. The children ran out of the SUV and then cautiously approached the deer. The deer was lifeless. Mikaela shrieked and began to sob. She kneeled down and put her hand on the deer's head.

"Mickey, don't touch it," her dad cautioned. Not listening to her father she continued to pat him on the head. She turned and looked toward the w est. She looked through the trees and could see a shimmer of light on the horizon. The horizon was orange but there were a few streaks of gold beaming through the trees. She pressed her hand firmly on the deer's head. Suddenly, the deer sprang up and darted into the forest.

"Ah, thank God, he was just stunned."

Mikaela looked at her father incredulously, not sure how he didn't know that it was she who had revived the stricken creature. The children filed back into the van and they were soon back home. Charlie helped Jayne into bed and the children played quietly near their mother's bed.

The next morning the children brought their mother breakfast-in-bed. She enjoyed the undercooked bacon and the soft-center pancakes. The children lay on the bed, watching her intently with each bite she took.

"Thanks kids. Why don't you go out and play."

The children gave their mother a hug and then ran outside. They started to play in the backyard and looked over the horizon toward Greta's house.

"Hey Zachary. Let's see if Greta's home."

Zachary nodded and they began to run through the fields toward her house. When they arrived they noticed the house seemed almost abandoned. It was the only house built on a small cul-de-sac and the end of a gravel road. All around were fields and marshes. It appeared to be the start of a neighborhood that was never finished apart from the very first house. As they walked around to the front of the house they could see the lawn had not been kept up. The grass was thick with weeds and the bushes were starting to grow over onto the covered porch. Walking up the stairs to the front door they listened intently to see if they could hear any signs of life. They rang the doorbell but there was no response. They knocked on the door and waited several minutes. Zachary peered into the front porch window.

"Boy, there doesn't seem to be much inside."

Mikaela walked over and began to look through the window.

"It's like it's been abandoned. I know she said she and her father had to go to Germany for a while, but she should have been back by now. This place looks like it has never been lived in."

The kids waited for another minute and then decided to run back home.

"Maybe she's in heaven?" Zachary asked. Mikaela shrugged her shoulders and suggested they go up to the attic. They played quietly waiting for the light to hit the ceilings windows just right. They waited and waited. As they continued to play, they noticed some clouds coming overhead; the formation was blocking the sunlight. It then started to lightly rain. Droplets of water soon softly pelted the windows. It was 4pm, the usual time that the sun would reveal the door. With the clouds however they realized that the door was not appearing. They stood up and walked over to where the door normally was. Mikaela began to push the wall but it was rigid and firm. There was no outline of a door.

"I guess we need the light for the door to appear?" Zachary asked.

The following month the children had waited for the sun to shine and reveal the door. It was now late October and it was getting colder. Mikaela noticed that the sun was lower in the sky. She began to realize that for the door to be revealed, the sun had to be high enough to shine directly on the window and that the sun itself had to appear in the window as they looked up. With winter approaching the sun was too low to provide direct sunlight on the ceiling windows.

As November went by, the children noticed a feeling of darkness over them. Their mother continued her new treatments but she didn't seem to get much better. Their father was noticeably absent. He said because of their mother not working he had to put more hours in at his job. Jake was absent as well and seldom at home. Their grandmother helped out but it was the children that often brought their mother her meals and would stay with her and talk. As the weather became more gloomy the children had a terrible feeling that they would never see heaven again.

CHAPTER 9

A Nasty Neighbor

At Christmas time the children had a brief respite from their depression. Their mother seemed to be doing better and their dad was spending more time at home. Jake seemed to be around more as well.

On Christmas Day the children opened their presents and were not disappointed. Mikaela received a tablet that was for her to do her homework, use to call for rides and have limited access to the internet. Zachary received a drone that he was only to use in the backyard. Unsure of what to get him, Charlie bought Jake a guitar and a couple hundred dollars-worth of music downloads to his phone. Jake was happy with the guitar and Charlie offered to provide him with some basic lessons. As soon as he progressed he would offer to pay for more advanced lessons at the local music store. Jake for the first time in a long time was excited about something. He dreamed of serenading Stella with his guitar. He also imagined himself the lead guitarist of the greatest rock band ever. It was a good day.

What made that Christmas Day one of the best for the Royaltons was that Jayne was up and sitting on the couch in front of the fire. Charlie made the dinner and the family was assembled around the table for the first time in a long time. They dined on smoked ham, mashed potatoes, green beans and salad. Charlie opened a bottle of champagne that he encouraged his wife to partake in.

"I really shouldn't Charlie, you know what the doctor said."

"I know dear but one glass will not hurt you."

Jayne complied with the request and the couple enjoyed a rare moment of bliss. Mikaela was happy to see her parents have a little bit of joy brought back into their lives. She felt there would be even more joy if she could find her way back to heaven. When would the sun be high enough to shine through the ceiling windows? She wondered with some anxiety. If she could be in heaven, she could be exposed to more of the Great Light. Surely that would help her mother she felt. She thought back to the day they had hit the deer. She remembered that when seeing the sun, a sense of power seem to surge through her and into the deer. The deer then immediately coming back to life and running away. Maybe she didn't need to go to heaven? Maybe she just needed to be positive and look to the light? Was that what Mother Light had taught her? A warmth seemed to fill her soul. A warmth she hadn't felt since the last day she had been in heaven. She now knew what she needed to do.

******

After Christmas break, Mikaela was determined to be a light unto the world. She was going to help as many people as possible. One of those people was an older woman she had seen several times that lived just down the street. She had met most of the people in the neighborhood and was now determined to introduce herself to this neighbor. She and Zachary walked down the street. Her home, like the others was old. This home however was very old. They thought they had heard somewhere that it was built during the Civil War and had been through several restorations.

When they arrived at the front steps, they proceeded slowly, creaking away as they did so. They looked into a large bay window that was next to the porch but it was completely dark. They neared the door and proceeded to use the large brass knocker which looked like it was about to fall off its hinges.

"Yes, how can I help you children?"

"Hi, my name is Mikaela Royalton and this is my brother Zachary. We live just down the street. We were just wondering if you need any help around your house?"

"Thank you children but that won't be necessary. I am able to work in the yard and fix things just fine."

"Oh, okay. Well, if you ever need anything, please let us know."

"I will sweetheart," the woman smiled and closed the door behind her. The children turned and ran to the next-door neighbor and asked if they needed anything. They did that for the rest of the afternoon.

While his siblings were out trying to help the world, Jake was doing a little research. He had been doing google searches for Stella Ashbury. He had tried to get her surname in the past but she wouldn't divulge. He did find her name printed on a folder in her duffel bag and so figured it must be it. Nothing seemed to come up in a search. He looked through the online yearbook at St. Pius high school but he could not find her there. Something seemed odd. He did another search to see if the name Stella was a nickname or short for something else. It appeared to be short for Estelle.

Jake then began to look through online maps of the east part of town, and like before when he had driven with his mom to the clinic, he could not locate any factories around there. He was starting to become troubled, wondering who it really was who lived in his basement. He decided to call the school directly and spoke with the receptionist. Due to privacy issues she could not give out any student information or whether Stella was a student there. Now he was really stumped. He would have to confront her and find out who she really was.

******

As the winter went along, Mikaela and Zachary tried to help their friends and neighbors as much as possible. Becky, whose father was now employed at Charlie's company was part of the new trio. Greta was still missing. Mikaela had checked with the school administration but they told her they could not divulge any information about other students to her. She really missed her friend and hoped she was okay. She would occasionally go over to the house to see if there were any signs of life but there were none. She assumed they had moved back to Germany.

The new trio of friends often went to the attic and started hanging various pieces of artwork and ornaments they had created. The place was really becoming their own. Their mother, given her condition, had seldom frequented her office since her cancer diagnosis. The place was now all their own. It was a great escape from all the worries of the world.

Along with all their various art projects, they also used the wall space to hang various pieces of schoolwork and assignments. They would hang a large poster of the multiplication tables and other learning aids such as a periodic table. The one that Mikaela kept looking at the most was a sun chart that tracked the sun's path across the horizon during the various solstices. She began to calculate at what point the sun might be high enough to fit within the frame of the ceiling windows. She kept a clipboard with a calendar on it and estimated that sometime in June the sun would be high enough to "hit the sweet spot."

"Mickey, why are you so interested in that chart?" Becky asked.

"Well, I noticed that when we last went to heaven, the sun beamed directly through the ceiling window revealing the portal."

"What?" Becky said with a look like Mikaela had just lost her mind.

"You know. When we went to heaven?"

"Heaven? When did we go to heaven?"

"You don't remember?"

Becky began to think. She did remember a really fun time with Mikaela and Zachary.

"That really happened? I thought it was dream!"

"No, it happened alright."

Becky looked at Mikaela and then to Zachary who gave a reassuring nod of the head.

"How do you think your dad got his job at my dad's company?"

Becky shook her head with a blank stare.

"The Great Light provided a job for your dad. Don't you remember the Great Light?"

Becky thought for a moment. Her facial expression soon turned from a complete look of confusion to exuberance when she realized what really had happened.

"I can't believe it. We were actually flying through the air?"

"We sure did!"

"Wow, let's do it again!"

"Well we can't. At least until the sun is high enough in the sky to show the portal."

Becky was confused. Her elation now turned to utter sadness as she drooped to the floor.

"I think in a couple of months we'll be able to go back."

This did not cheer Becky up. The children continued to quietly play in the attic.

****

When Spring arrived, the children started to become more hopeful of their next trip to heaven. For now they would have to continue to be patient. On the first Saturday morning of April, there was a knock on the front door. Charlie opened it and there stood a solemn older lady. It was the neighbor from down the street who Mikaela and Zachary had offered help to.

"Good morning. My name is Eileen Harrell. I live just down the road."

"Good to meet you Mrs. Harrell. I'm Charlie Royalton. How can I help you?"

"Well, your children were so good to come to my house a while back and offered to help me. I was wondering if I could take then up on their offer."

"Sure, what did you need help with?"

"Well, I sort of threw my back out the other day gardening and I was needing a little help with pulling out some weeds from my backyard. I can pay them."

"I'm sure the kids will love to help you. You don't need to pay them. I'll send them over once they've had their breakfast."

"Thank you so much."

Charlie closed the door and watched Mrs. Harrell walk down the street. He could tell she was older but moved in a brisk manner.

Once the children had finished their breakfast they ran over to Mrs. Harrell's house. Mrs. Harrell greeted them at the front door and then instructed them to go around to the backyard. She gave them a trowel and garbage bag each for the weeds. The children had never done any garden work before. Jayne had always loved to work in the yard by herself so this was the first attempt they had made at it. The morning had been a little cool but soon the sun was shining and the children were enjoying being bathed in the sunlight. Mrs. Harrell watched the children from the back porch. After a couple of hours, Mrs. Harrell brought the children two large glasses of lemonade.

"How are you progressing my dears?"

"Pretty well, I think. Does it look okay?"

"Yes, I think you're doing a great job!" Mrs. Harrell smiled knowing that not a lot of work had been done, but it was sufficient for a ten and eight-year-old.

"When you get to the flowerbed over there, just make sure you only pull weeds and not flowers."

Mikaela turned to study the flowerbed and began to wonder what were flowers and what were weeds. When they were weeding the field it seemed easy to identify the weeds. They had thorny looking leaves with yellow crowns. But when she looked in the flowerbed there seemed to be all kinds of flowers mixed with all kinds of grass and leafy plants. It looked like it hadn't been touched in years.

"Ah, Mrs. Harrell, which are the weeds?"

With a perturbed expression on her face, Mrs. Harrell got up from her chair on the porch and walked over to Mikaela.

"See all those scraggly looking green leafy plants."

"Yes."

"Do you see those purple ones?"

"Yes. Those aren't flowers?"

"Yes, but they are wild violets and they can be bad for the gladiolus."

Mikaela nodded her head, trying to figure out how she was going to know which was which. Zachary gave Mikaela a long look, also wondering how they were going to figure out how they would proceed. Mikaela looked at the sun that was now brightly shining down on the entire yard. As Mrs. Harrell napped in her chair, Mikaela and Zachary slowly pushed their way through the weeds and flowers in the flowerbed. They proceeded slowly and pulled what they thought were weeds with great care as if playing the game of "Operation" that they so loved to do.

After thirty minutes of their careful pruning, Mrs. Harrell came running around to the flowerbed. She looked like she had seen a ghost.

"What are you doing?!!! You've ruined my flowerbed. Get out of there!!!"

The children were stunned and stood frozen.

"Get out of here, I don't need you tearing up my flowerbed!!!"

The children had never been yelled at like that before. They couldn't even remember a time when they had ever been yelled at. They looked at each other in horror and then immediately ran home. They ran up the stairs of the front porch and quickly pushed through the front door, running as fast as they could into the kitchen. There was no one there so they decided to run upstairs to their mother.

"Mom, mom, I think we did something wrong!!!" Mikaela frantically cried.

"What's the matter kids?" Jayne said as the two jumped into her arms.

"We ruined Mrs. Harrell's flower garden!!!" a teary-eyed Zachary exclaimed.

"Mom, I'm so sorry, I thought Mrs. Harrell was telling us to remove the wild violets from her flowerbed and I guess we removed the wrong kind of flowers. She was ready to kill us!!!"

"Who is Mrs. Harrell and why were you in her flowerbed?"

"I told the kids to help her," Charlie said as he walked into the bedroom.

"She's the older woman down the street. She came to me this morning asking if the kids could help her. I guess she asked them to do some weeding," Charlie said apologetically looking at the children.

"I thought her head was about to pop off when she looked at the flower bed," Zachary said, still trembling from the experience.

"Don't worry guys. You didn't know. I'll go over to Mrs. Harrell's house and ask her if I can fix it. Worse comes to worse I'll buy her some new flowers."

The children took solace that their dad would intervene. It was the first time in a long, long while that Mikaela felt that she had done something wrong. Whether at home, school or on the soccer field she was usually praised. This was quite disconcerting to her.

"Honey, don't worry about it. Daddy will take care of it."

"Mom, I'm sorry, I was really trying hard to follow her directions."

"Don't fret yourself. Sometimes thing do not always go right. You're such a brilliant kid and you are not used to things not going the right way. Mistakes are fine, we all learn from them. Anyway, don't worry about it. Go clean yourselves off and I'll go bake some cookies."

The children were happy that their mother had the strength to get out of bed and do something a little more normal. Maybe it was a sign she was getting better. Or maybe it was just a mother trying to do something nice for her children. Whatever it was it was a nice change.

After cleaning up and having cookies, the children went upstairs to the attic. Before they went into the attic Mikaela peered down the street looking toward Mrs. Harrell's house. She shuddered thinking about the events of the day. They went into the attic where Zachary starting playing with his toy cars. Mikaela got a book on flowers and began to study them intently. She never wanted to make the mistake of not knowing what was a flower versus a weed. As she read, she liked looking at all the beautiful flowers and plants. She started to think that she might like to be a biologist or a botanist one day.

******

Several weeks later, the much-anticipated day of the sun's favorable path over the ceiling windows had arrived, or so hoped the children. They waited and waited. Finally around 3pm they could see some of the direct rays of the sun starting to beam through the window. They anxiously waited for more light to spill in and shine on the back wall of the attic. As the year before, the light twinkled and began to cover the back wall. As it did so the portal revealed itself. The children, feeling like they had waited a thousand years, ran as fast as they could to the door, pulled the rope and opened the door. Like before there was the heavenly expanse and the long beautiful green field they had run in previously. They frantically ran through the door and then jumped into the air, flying like fighter jets zooming through the air. As with their very first visit, they descended down through the waterfall and played in and under the water. The bubbles felt like millions of tiny cushions rubbing on their faces. With each second they were back in heaven, their strength increased and their sense of love and security enveloped them like a wonderful, cozy blanket. It was home.

After they played for a while, they could feel themselves being called by Mother Light. The children quickly darted over to the temple and could see Mother Light, beaming with love and joy on their return.

"Children, it is so good to see you again. We have missed you."

"Yes, Mother Light, we wanted to come sooner but it seems we can only come here when the sun is high enough to beam through the ceiling windows into our attic."

"Yes, that is true. Remember, your world is only a representation of what is in our world. There are limitations. Mankind has placed those limitations on themselves. Most are not interested in the true world, the world of light. Consequently they live in darkness, in shadows and there are limits to what they can do. As you have seen when you come here, there are no limits. Now do you know why you were allowed to come here?"

The children shook their heads in unison.

"You are children. Good and kind children and you are pure of heart. You do not want to live in your world but in heaven. It is in your nature. But when people grow up, they lose their innocence, their purity of heart. They wish to continue to stumble in the darkness. They want to follow their own path and not the path that leads them to the Great Light."

"But that's silly Mother Light. Why would anyone not want to live here?"

"Pride. They don't want to follow the light. They want to create their own light, their own world where they are in charge, where they have the control. But by wanting that type of world they become enslaved, they are in fact, not in the least bit in control. And when you apply all the wonderful things that the light provides, it brings happiness, life, health, true family with a mother and father raising children. The world rejects these things and so darkness and confusion reigns. What the world deems as good to them is evil, and what is evil is deemed by them as good."

"How can we help people Mother Light?"

"I know it will be difficult, but there will come a time, for a while, when you will not be able to enter heaven. The reason is because you have a purpose on Earth. You need to continue to help people, even if those people do not want help, you must help them."

"How long do we have to do that?"

"You will need to spend the rest of your human life on Earth helping others. There will come a time when you will have families, grow old and then you will become part of the Great Light."

"Can't we just bring our family and friends now…not wait for death?"

"There is nothing to fear from death. Death is only a transition to becoming who you really are."

"But why did the Earth exist in the first place? Why didn't we just start off in heaven?"

"That was the plan, however plans change. There were creatures who started in heaven. They didn't want to stay in heaven, they wanted their own world. The Great Light created for them their own world. These creatures became human beings and their world became Earth."

"But what about the Big Bang and evolution and all that?"

"What your scientists on Earth are seeing is the result of that creation. When the Great Light created the Earth, the universe came into life in another dimension. In that dimension, the Great Light created the universe you know by mixing light with various elements and there was a great explosion creating an expanding universe. Much like breathing into a balloon; life was breathed into that dimension and now you have the galaxies the solar system; everything that mankind wanted."

"So mankind wanted to be placed into their own dimension?"

"Yes, humans want to be in control of their own world, so one was given to them. They now have exactly what they wanted. Unfortunately, that world is dying and is corrupt. There were humans that wanted things so badly that they were willing to kill for them. People soon were lying, cheating and stealing things that were not theirs. Taking things and swindling things from others. There was lust for sex, lust for money and there was soon no love in them, only pride, only desire for themselves and how they could satisfy themselves. Here in heaven, only those who think about others can thrive. Only when we think about a greater good a greater love can one truly live."

"I understand Mother Light. We only want to do good, we only want to help others."

"That is why you are here my children. That is why you need to go back to Earth. You will be able to come here a few more times, but eventually the portal will close. In the meantime you can come here and learn."

"Okay, Mother Light we will listen and do good."

"But remember children, there are many people who do not want your help. There are many that will make fun of you because of what you believe. It is important to always think of me and the Great Light and we will help you through the rough times."

Mikaela began to think of the people in her life who had rejected her help like Mrs. Harrell. Life on Earth was not going to be easy, especially as she grew older.

"Now children, before you go back to Earth, there is someone I would like you to meet."

From the horizon they could see an orb zooming toward them. Like the five friendly orbs they had met before, they could see a young, happy being. This one appeared to be a young man."

"Hello children. My name is Phillip Harris. You might know me as "cranky old Mr. Harris," the man said with a buoyancy.

"Mr. Harris? Aren't you the gentleman who used to live in the neighborhood by our school…?"

"Who used to threaten anyone that came on your property with a shotgun?"

"That's the one."

The children were stunned. He looked so different from what they remembered. He was an old man that walked with a limp, with gray hair and a bald head. He wore old smelly clothes and was the most crotchety person anyone could meet. How did he end up in heaven? He was completely transformed. It was like he was twenty years old.

"Now children, you have to do me a favor. Your brother Jake is in a bad state and it could get worse. He did a silly thing by agreeing with a couple of other boys to burgle my house. When I caught them and followed them out of my house, I took a shot at them. That was not a good thing I did, and I paid for it. It knocked me over and I had a heart attack and died. By the grace and mercy of the Great Light I am here today. The Great Light can see everything and knows what is in our hearts. I had for a long time helped people. I had volunteered at homeless shelters, gave of my income to help the needy, but one day, I guess I lost my vision of what I needed to do. I mistakenly felt that people were trying to take advantage of me, that helping others wasn't important. I lost sight of what was good, so don't follow my mistake. Don't become grumpy. There are times in your life when you will ask what is the point of helping others. Don't give up, keep helping others.

Anyway, going back to your brother. Please tell him that my death was not his fault. The Great Light was summoning me anyway and I am so happy it did. Please encourage him. Tell him he is not guilty of what happened. He is being troubled right now; troubled by darkness, troubled by other individuals. There are individuals who are telling him they are his friends but they really are not. You need to help him. You need to be there for Jake and for your mother."

The children, still stunned by the revelation, nodded their heads. Mother Light bid them farewell and they were soon in the air headed back to their house.

******

The next day at school, the usual clan of girls assembled at the cafeteria to have lunch. The chatter started with soccer, boys and which teacher had the hardest class. As they were finishing up on how Mr. Waring was a "psycho drill sergeant," Greta walked in. Mikaela, seeing her good friend dropped everything and ran over to her to give her a hug.

"Greta, where have you been?!!! I've missed you."

"Me too Mickey. Sorry, my dad had to take a trip back to Germany."

"We went over to your house the other day and it looked vacant."

"Yeah, we're not living there anymore. My dad wanted to live closer to the university so we moved to an apartment near campus."

"Oh, that's too bad. I wanted to see your house again and play over there."

"Sorry."

"Anyway, it's good to have you back!"

"It's good to be back."

"Will he have to go back to Germany soon?"

"No, he said he was done for a while. We might go back at Christmas to see our family."

Mikaela was so happy to have her friend back. She adored her brother Zachary but there were times she just wanted another girl her age around. The girls continued to talk about what was going on in their lives.

"Hey Mattie, how come you don't come over to my house anymore?" Mikaela asked.

"Sorry Mickey but I've been grounded by my parents. My grades are not great, so I have go home right after school and work on my homework."

"You look stressed out."

"I am. My dad just moved out. My parents are getting a divorce."

"Mattie, I am so sorry to hear that," Mikaela said as she got up from her seat and immediately walked over and gave Mattie a big hug.

"Wow, that's a bummer Mattie, but hey that's the way it goes. My parents divorced years ago," a rather jaded Brittany said.

"That's why I am telling you guys. Family is the most important thing. If there is not a mother at home and a father providing there is too much stress on a family. Society is falling apart and it's because everyone wants to do their own thing."

"Ok, calm down you weirdo."

"She's not weird. She's right," a rather timid Becky interjected.

"What do you know about it Becky?"

"My dad just got a job at Mickey's dad's company. He is so happy now. My parents are really getting along. My mom was able to quit her job and is home full-time now. She couldn't be happier."

"Well that's lame. There's no way I'm going to quit my job for some guy."

"Well, good luck having a family Brittany."

While the girls continued their discussion, an interloper by the name of Ms. Lambert had been passing by and had heard Mikaela's declaration on the family. She immediately headed to Principal Wilson's office to relay what she had heard.

After going back to class, Mikaela was greeted by Mr. Waring at the doorway.

"Mikaela. Go to the principal's office. She wants to speak with you."

Becky gave Mikaela an astonished look. Mikaela herself was quite surprised and wondered what in the world the principal wanted. She had hoped there was nothing going on with her mother. She walked briskly into the office and was greeted by the receptionist who sent her through to the principal's office. Mikaela had never been in the principal's office before and walked in like it was hallowed ground. It seemed dark and a little depressing. The air felt thick, like maybe there were no fans on to help with circulation.

"Mikaela, please come in," Principal Wilson said in a gruff voice. Principal Barbara Wilson was a tall, intimidating figure who was an ex-marine. She was a no-nonsense educator much like Mr. Waring.

"I've been told by one of the teachers that you are spreading a rather disturbing message to the other students."

Mikaela's heart began to race and she started to feel nervous. What was she being accused of?

"I'm sorry Principal Wilson, what message have I been spreading?"

"A message of hate. You know that in this state and really the entire country it is unlawful for hate speech."

"I still don't understand Principal Wilson, what hate speech have I been spreading?"

"The idea that there can only be one family. A relationship between a man and woman only."

"I merely said that the most important thing is to have a family. The most important job for a woman is to be a mother and the most important job for a man is to be a father."

"Well, that is ludicrous. I don't know who told you that but we live in a different age. That type of thinking is antiquated and dangerous."

"It's dangerous to want to have a family?"

"No, it's dangerous to say it is the most important thing for a woman to be a mother."

"Why?"

"Mikaela, you are young and you don't understand yet, but the most important thing for a woman to do is to be her own individual. She is not defined by any specific job or occupation, but she should be free to pursue anything she wants. There was a time when women were forced to be wives and mothers and that is the only thing they could be. They couldn't work. They couldn't do anything outside of the home. In some Middle Eastern countries that is still true today. But because of the hard work of other women, you now enjoy rights today that many women never had. You can be anything you want to be."

"Maybe I can be anything I want to be, but it still doesn't change the fact that the most important thing to be is a mother. To have a family. To raise children and educate them."

"And if you are just a mother, what will you educate them on?"

"Everything; reading, writing, arithmetic. But much more than that. I will educate them on life. How to be a good person. How to help others."

"So you think you are a good person?"

Mikaela stopped to think. She knew that most people believed it to be arrogance to call one's self good.

"Yes. Yes I do," she said with great confidence. Confidence that took Principal Wilson aback.

"And what is it that you do that makes you good?"

"Loving others. Loving others more than myself."

The principal sat back in her chair and began to rock back and forth.

"I like you Mikaela, I think you are a bright girl. However, I do not want you promoting these ideas any longer. If I hear you preaching these beliefs, I will be forced to suspend you from school."

Mikaela was in shock. Why was she being threatened with expulsion for her beliefs? She took a breath and then spoke.

"I guess you better suspend me now then because I have no desire to change what I believe or stopping telling others."

"Very well. You leave me with no choice. I will call your parents and let them know and they will need to come and pick you up."

Back at the house, Jake was staring at his mother through the open bedroom door. She was sleeping. He felt a pain in his soul as he watched her. He remembered his mother as being so vibrant, so loving and caring, always so energetic. And now, to see her almost lifeless was too much to bear. He began to think that her health decline was because of him, because of the evil he had been doing. Maybe he should give up his pursuits of pleasure and release and focus on his mother? But as he thought about the pain his mother was going through, he wanted release all that much more.

When Charlie arrived at Mikaela's school, he immediately headed to the principal's office and walked passed the receptionist.

"Principal Wilson, what seems to be the problem?" Charlie said in an agitated voice.

"Mr. Royalton, we have a problem with your daughter. She is not willing to comply with our rules and regulation against hate speech."

"Hate speech? My daughter doesn't have a hateful bone in her body. She's the kindest soul I know."

"Yes, well, she's going around advocating for families with one mother and one father only."

"Yeah, so? What's wrong with that?"

"At this school we are inclusive of all families Mr. Royalton. Not just one type of family."

Charlie Royalton looked at Principal Wilson with astonishment. He then looked at his daughter. She looked at him with moist, but hopeful eyes. He then motioned to the principal to walk toward the corner of the room away from Mikaela. He started whispering to the principal. Mikaela tried to listen but could not make out what they were saying. Principal Wilson nodded to Charlie and then walked over to Mikaela. She motioned in silence for Mikaela to go with her father. The father and daughter departed the principal's office and got into Charlie's pick-up truck across the street.

"Did I do something wrong dad?"

"No honey. People are just sensitive these days about what you can say. Maybe just try and keep things to your friends."

"I thought I did. I have no idea how the principal knew about what we were talking about at lunch time."

"Don't worry about it my love," Charlie gave Mikaela a reassuring look. Mikaela began to study her father. She loved her father but had noticed he seemed a little distant lately. He was spending more time at work. Her mother said it was in an effort to make more money since she was no longer working. That might be the case but there did seem like something was different with her father. She couldn't quite figure out what.

CHAPTER 10

Fireworks of a Different Sort

On July 4th, the family celebrated both the birthday of the country as well as that of Mikaela. Mikaela always like the fact that her birthday was on July 4th. It made her proud to be an American, plus it gave the added bonus of fireworks on her special day. For the first time in a long time the house was buzzing with activity. Becky's mother Melissa was over helping with the party since Jayne was still recuperating from another treatment session. All of Mikaela's friends were over and were having a great time. Charlie had fixed up the backyard with streamers, flags, posters and various other decorations celebrating both the 4th of July and Mikaela.

The children were having fun in the backyard; playing soccer and blasting music as loud as they could. Charlie had the barbeque out and fired up to cook the kids hotdogs and hamburgers. Charlie and Melissa had moved a couch upstairs into the master bedroom right by the bay window so that Jayne could look down on the festivities below.

Jake, after spending the morning in the basement with Stella, snuck her out to the basecamp so they could be away from the family and enjoy the fireworks in another part of town. It would also be Stella's first encounter with the rest of the Black Knights.

After lunch, the tribe of girls plus Zachary assembled at a large picnic table and began to distribute gifts to Mikaela.

"Open mine Mickey!!!" shouted Brittany. Brittany came from a wealthy family and she was known for letting everyone know about it. Mikaela excitedly opened the large box which produced a large barn for her Magic Pony figurines. The other girls knew it would be hard to top that present. After going through the rest of her gifts, the magic moment had arrived – cake!!! Charlie came down from the kitchen with a large chocolate cake practically set ablaze with candles. Everyone bellowed Happy Birthday and Mikaela stood proud as the cake was set down before her. She felt like a queen. She looked up to the master bedroom window and could see the faint outline of her mother's face. She smiled and made a little wave.

"Okay birthday girl, make a wish and blow out all the candles," Charlie shouted over the blare of the music.

Mikaela closed her eyes. She began to think about heaven and how she wished she could bring all of her friends and family there. She hoped her wish would come true. She opened her eyes and then blew as hard as she could, getting every last candle. She was pleased with the result. Charlie quickly walked over and began slicing pieces of cake and handing them out to the ravenous girls. Once the cake had been consumed, Charlie encourage the girls to burn off the sugar with another game of soccer. The girls complied and another frenzy of activity began.

As the game continued, it soon drew someone who was not a fan; Mrs. Harrell. Mrs. Harrell stormed over and began to yell at Charlie about the volume of the music. The girls stopped their game to look at the confrontation.

"Mr. Royalton do you have any idea how loud that is?"

"Sorry Mrs. Harrell, we will turn it down." Charlie immediately ran over to the boombox and turned down the volume. Given the other noise in the neighborhood and the much louder explosions to come that day, Charlie was a bit surprised that Mrs. Harrell would be so concerned. He ran back over to Mrs. Harrell who stood with a look of condemnation.

"Is that better?" a rather timid Charlie asked.

"That will do, but please keep it down."

Charlie nodded and dare not flinch. He felt her eying him up and down like he was a serviceman being inspected by a drill sergeant. She eventually took her eyes off of him and began to look around the backyard. The girls were also intimidated and did not want to make any false moves. Beyond her stern expression, Mrs. Harrell was also fit and quite tall, an imposing figure. No one would want to cross paths with Mrs. Harrell. For Mikaela, that already happened and she didn't want it to happen again. Eventually Mrs. Harrell relented and turned to walk home. Charlie noticed that she stopped by the basement window and began to peer in.

"Boy, she's a nosey one," Charlie said under his breath. Immediately Mikaela grabbed his hand. He looked down at her and could see she was disturbed by Mrs. Harrell's appearance. Her cheeks looked red and she was out of breath.

"It's okay honey, she's leaving."

Mikaela looked at Charlie with an expression he had never seen from his daughter before, it was utter fear. Mikaela had always been a happy, confident girl, but for the first time he saw her as vulnerable. When Mikaela looked at Mrs. Harrell leaving, she could see her surrounded in darkness. There was no soul to Mrs. Harrell.

At basecamp, Mac, Will, Jake and Stella gathered. Jake introduced Stella to the other boys. The boys were immediately smitten. Stella was wearing short, tight cut-off jean shorts with a very tight white t-shirt that left little to the imagination. Mac got the proceedings rolling with the official lighting of the first joint. Stella seemed to take to marijuana like she had been an old pro. Given her background Jake could see why she would need the soothing effects of cannabis.

"So Stella, I hear you go to St. Pius? Great party school," Mac said with a knowing smile.

"Yeah, pretty crazy over there."

"Pretty strict, I hear," Will offered.

"It is strict, they make them wear uniforms. Stella has to wear a plaid skirt every day."

"Oooh, I'd like to see that. I hope it's a short one," Mac said with a crafty smile.

"Oh, it is short. I purposely wear it short. But you wouldn't be able to handle it," Stella said as she blew a stream of smoke from her mouth. The boys were mesmerized. This was a woman of the world.

"Hey, I'm no kid," Mac said.

"How old are you?"

"I'm sixteen but turning seventeen next month."

"You're just a boy."

"I'm a man. You're just a slut."

It happened in a split second. Stella seemed to almost levitate from the ground. She went to where Mac was seated and punched him hard in the face. Mac was completely flattened, landing on his back. The other two boys were stunned. Jake knew from previous encounters that Stella was strong, but didn't truly understand how strong. As Mac lay lifeless, the other two boys tried to revive him while Stella sat calmly taking hits off of a joint. Eventually Mac recovered but he was weary of saying anything to Stella for the rest of the day. Jake himself was a little guarded. He considered Stella his girlfriend but hadn't fully understood her power. While it was still a day and age where men were generally considered stronger than women because of their size, it was light years from the times where women were considered the "weaker sex." Truth of it is, from an emotional, intellectual and in many cases physical standpoint, men were the weaker sex. Jake soon realized that was the truth, and he would approach his intimacy with Stella a little more cautiously in future.

Back at the house at Arendelle Court, everyone was settling into their chairs to watch the fireworks. There was an unobstructed view from the backyard over the field. Beyond the field was a large lake with a small island. The fireworks would be launched from the island. As the sky turned dark orange, then purple and then black, the children started getting louder and more rambunctious in anticipation of the show. Slowly several small flares arced their way through the sky, leading to sparkles and small explosions. What they wanted though was to go straight to the loud explosions, especially the ones that would crackle and pop and then go boom!!! With each launch the girls oohed and awed.

Near the field behind the Royalton's, Jake took Stella to sit with a blanket to watch the fireworks. There was a small wooded area near the marsh where they could be hidden. Jake had a bundle of blankets they could use for pillows and one large one to lie on. They too enjoyed the night sky as it seemed to explode. The fireworks made Stella feel romantic and the couple kissed more than observed the festivities.

After the fireworks ended, Charlie escorted all the girls home. Most of them lived in the neighborhood and a few he had to drive to other parts of town. Mikaela waited for her dad to return to thank him for all he had done that day but he didn't return. She went to bed thinking about him. Lately it seemed he would go out late at night and not return until the early morning. Occasionally, when she got up to use the bathroom in the early morning, she would hear her father moving about the house, sometimes coming in through the front door. Where was he going? Shouldn't he be home with her mother? His behavior was becoming more and more a mystery.

As Stella and Jake lay in the field, the fireworks having long ceased, they became quite amorous, especially Stella. It had been a warm day and now that things had cooled slightly, she made her move. She grabbed him by the shirt and he knew what would soon be happening. She began to tear at the buttons on his shirt. *Are we about to have sex?* Jake said to himself trying to control his emotions, but wanting to scream to the world that he was no longer going to be a virgin.

"Hey, you're ripping the but…"

She clamped her hand down over his mouth.

"Shhhhhhh! Hey, I'll buy you a new shirt."

She then pulled off the t-shirt that was under his dress shirt..

"Just relax," she said as he went to try and remove her t-shirt. She pushed him down onto the blanket with the force of a professional wrestler and pinned him down. She kissed his neck and face and then moved to his chest and stomach. She looked like a possessed animal. The feeling was excruciatingly sweet and he felt he might pass out. When Jake looked at Stella, she seemed to have the eyes of a wild cat, ablaze with fire. She appeared to be something other than human. Was she some other entity? He had often wondered why such a beautiful girl had been with him. As the two continued their passionate embrace, Jake could feel Stella squeezing him. He could feel her heartbeat pounding as she lay on top of him. Stella seemed to be moving in concert with the sounds around her, alive like some jungle cat.

"Hey, what are you two doing there?!!!"

Their hearts already pounding, Jake and Stella turned to see Mrs. Harrell standing nearby. She looked like she was in the marsh, obstructed by the weeds as if she had been crouching down.

"What are you doing here?" Jake challenged her.

"This is my land and you are trespassing!"

"I'm pretty sure this is either our land or public property," Jake contested. Stella stood up and grabbed Jake by the arm. She urged him that the two should just leave. Jake was angry that the "grumpy old woman down the street" was interrupting what would have been his initiation into the world of sex. How could she have the right to break up his journey into manhood! He was indignant and would never forgive Mrs. Harrell for what she had down.

Once convinced the teenagers were leaving, Mrs. Harrell grunted and began to walk on a path that would lead around to the back of her house. Jake occasional turned to check her progress. When they reached the basement, Stella gave him a kiss and told him she was too tired and wanted to go to sleep. This made Jake even more furious and vowed to somehow get back at Mrs. Harrell.

******

The next morning, Mikaela arose early to see if her mother needed anything. She went down to the kitchen to make a bowl of oatmeal. As she went down she noticed her father sleeping on a couch in the spare bedroom on the first floor. He was still wearing the clothes from the day before.

After making her mother a bowl of oatmeal, Mikaela walked it up to her room. As she entered the room she found her mother laying on the floor near the bathroom.

"Mom!!! What happened?!!!" Mikaela yelled, dropping the bowl of oatmeal on the floor as she ran to her mother. She kneeled next to her mother, running her hand over her forehead, trying to revive her. She ran to the doorway and yelled for her father. Charlie quickly ran up the stairs and into the bedroom.

"My God, what happened?"

"I think she passed out."

"Jayne, Jayne, are you okay?!!!" a frantic Charlie yelled to her, hoping for any signs of life. Charlie grabbed Jayne's lifeless body and placed her onto the bed. He grabbed her wrist trying to ascertain a pulse. Not knowing what to do, Mikaela brought a wet towel from the bathroom to place on her mother's forehead.

"What's the matter? What's wrong with mom?" Zachary yelled having just come into the room. Ignoring Zachary, Charlie called for an ambulance. Jayne was alive but was breathing heavily and not responsive. Her face seemed to be turning blue.

"Please God, don't take her now!" came the plea from a horrified Charlie. The children got onto the bed with their mother and tried to revive her. Zachary clutched onto her arm. When the ambulance arrived, the EMTs raced upstairs to prep her and place her on a stretcher. They took her vital signs and she seemed to be drifting away. Charlie, Mikaela and Zachary were in hot pursuit of the medics who were rushing Jayne down the stairs on the stretcher, quickly placing her in the ambulance. They roared off with the siren blaring as the rest of the family hopped into the SUV and followed them down the street. They arrived at the hospital five minutes later.

Back at the house, Jake, having just awoken from his long night, called out. The house seemed deadly quiet. He walked down the hallway to the master bedroom to see his mother but only found the disheveled bed. He called out again but there was no one. As he headed downstairs, he received a call on his cell from his father telling him to come over to the hospital right away. He jumped into the old beater his dad had recently fixed up for him and headed over to the hospital. He found his father and siblings in the waiting room.

"Dad, what's going on?"

"Your mother is having some issues," he said with tears in his eyes.

"I don't know if it's a stroke or what it is. They just rushed her into the ER."

It was another couple of hours before a doctor finally came into the waiting room to give an update on what was happening to Jayne.

"Are you the Royaltons?"

Charlie nodded to the doctor who appeared to be in his late fifties with gray hair and balding at the top. He looked in good shape though and gave an air of confidence and experience. Exactly what they needed at the moment.

"You wife and mother suffered a minor stroke. She is in surgery right now. They are finishing up but she should be fine. They performed at mechanical thrombectomy."

"What is that doctor?" Mikaela asked with a hopeful expression.

"The doctors insert a catheter into a large blood vessel inside the head. The catheter is a device to pull the blood clot out of the vessel – that is what caused your mother's stroke."

"But how did happen in the first place?"

"It's hard to say. Her body has been going through a lot. If there is inactivity like she has been having, that could be the cause. When she gets better you will need to figure out a way to get her some exercise."

The doctor continued to explain everything that happened and the best way for the family on how to plan and deal with Jaynes recuperation. The family debated about staying but felt that being only ten minutes away they could be at her bedside quickly. It was best for now to let her rest.

When they arrived back home, Mikaela waited for Jake to arrive while Charlie and Zachary went inside. Mikaela walked up to Jake as he pulled in, giving him a bright smile like she had done so at the hospital.

"You okay Jake?"

Jake nodded with a tired look on his face. He looked like he had been through a lot.

"Before you go in, I want to talk to you."

Jake was slightly taken aback. The two had never really connected, at least for a very long time. He gave her a long look but then relented and walked over to the front porch, sitting on the top step.

"I know you have been going through a lot with school and stuff, but I want you to know you can talk to me. I may be a lot younger than you but I have learned a lot over the past year, especially with everything that's happened to mom. I just want you to know that if you ever want to talk to me, you can."

Jake stared at Mikaela for a while. He did see some maturity in her. She had always been the star of the family so he had been a bit resentful of her. Maybe she was someone he could confide in? He had been holding so much in. There was very little he could tell the Black Knights as far as what he was truly feeling. And with Stella, it was also difficult to share what he thought. She was someone who was quite worldly – she seemed to have experience beyond her years. She knew so many more things than he did. For being only a year older, she seemed too advanced for him.

"Thanks Mikaela. I appreciate your concern. I think though I need someone a little older to talk to."

"That's fine. Maybe you can talk with your friends, or maybe dad?"

"I don't know about dad. He seems a little distant these days."

"You noticed that too? I thought it was just me."

"I haven't been talking to him a lot lately, but when I do I can tell his mind is on other things."

"I know what you mean. He used to always want to talk to me, want to know what was going on with me. Now he never talks unless I talk to him first."

"He must be going through a lot with mom being sick."

"Yeah, I think you're right. How's school going?"

"Ah, it's okay. I'm glad it's summertime. Next year though I may need to go to summer school."

"Maybe I can help you?"

Jake gave Mikaela a strange look like she was out of her mind.

"No, that's okay. You worry about your own stuff and I'll take care of mine."

"Speaking of your own stuff, I wanted to let you know that Mr. Harris is fine."

Now Jake gave her a look like she had really gone completely insane.

"What are you talking about?"

"You know Mr. Harris, the one that died several months ago. He has forgiven you."

Jake stood up and peered down at his sister like she was a lunatic. He shook his head and walked into the house. He ran upstairs to his room and slammed the door behind him, flopping on top of his bed. He began to sob thinking about the old man and that he might be responsible for his death. He then thought about his sister. How in the world did she know about Mr. Harris? Did she know that he was possibly responsible for his death? She said that Mr. Harris had forgiven him. *How in the hell could she know that?* He was starting to believe that maybe Mikaela was quite special as the rest of the family did.

******

The following day, the family went to the hospital to see Jayne. She was sitting up in bed and was so happy to see her family. The doctor came in and told them that they wanted to observe her for one more day and then they would be sending her home. The children were thrilled.

Later that day, when the family got home from the hospital, Mikaela and Zachary decided to ride their bicycles into town. They wanted to buy some candy at one of the convenience stores. On the way there they noticed a young man sitting in the stoop of a doorway. It looked like an old beaten down shop of some sort that was closed or abandoned. The young man looked like he was asleep. It appeared to be an odd place to be sleeping and he was slumped to one side looking very uncomfortable and shivering. Mikaela became concerned that he might need help.

"Hello, mister. Are you okay?"

The young man slowly lifted his head. He looked like he was in a daze. He nodded his head and then slumped further down. His clothing was disheveled and smelling and it looked like he was intoxicated. He appeared to be no more than twenty years old.

"You look like you might need help?"

Zachary nudged his sister like he thought it would be a good idea to leave him alone. Mikaela looked toward the sun that was breaking through some clouds. She began to think about what to do. Clearly this young man was in trouble.

"C'mon, Mikaela, let's go," an impatient Zachary kept urging her.

"Ok, but we have to make a stop first." Zachary reluctantly agreed and they got on their bikes and peddled toward downtown. As they reached Main Street, Mikaela headed to an older building with a red brick façade. It was one of the original buildings from the 1800's that had been renovated along with the rest of the downtown area ten years earlier. The building had now become a homeless shelter. Mikaela and Zachary parked their bikes and then walked inside. There were quite a few homeless people inside; mostly men but many single mothers with children as well.

"Can I help you children?" a kindly gentleman asked.

"Yes, there's a young man down the road who needs a place to stay. Can you help me bring him over here?"

The man was surprised by Mikaela's thoughtfulness and concern.

"Ah sure. Why don't we get my truck and we'll drive over to him."

Mikaela and Zachary got into his truck and they drove down the road to find him. They soon spotted the young man and pulled over to the side of the street. The man from the homeless shelter got out and walked over to the young man with Mikaela and Zachary following closely behind.

"Young man. How about you come with me? We have a nice warm place for you to stay with food and other necessities."

The young man looked up at him and shook his head.

"You planning on living here?"

"Please go away. I have a headache."

"C'mon son. You can't stay out here all day. The cops are probably going to make you leave anyway."

"Then let 'em take me. I don't care."

The man from the homeless shelter looked at Mikaela and shrugged his shoulders. Mikaela smiled and then walked up to the young man. She put her hand on his shoulder. As she did so, a ray of light beamed down on them.

"Mister. I know you are hurting right now. But you have to know that you have a purpose in life. Maybe that's hard to see right now but you do. But the first thing you need to do is get yourself a place to stay…get cleaned-up…get fed. Let's go with this man. They will also be able to help you get a job and any necessary training, education that you need."

The man from the homeless shelter was duly impressed with Mikaela. For a young girl she seemed to know a lot about homeless shelters.

"Alright, as long you stop bugging me about it."

Mikaela and the man from the homeless shelter helped get the young man to his feet. They then escorted him over to the pick-up truck and they were soon heading for the homeless shelter. When they arrived, Mikaela and Zachary watched as the young man got settled in. They introduced themselves to the kindly gentleman who helped the young man.

"I'm Mikaela and this is my brother Zachary."

"Good to meet you Mikaela and Zachary. I'm Walt. I want thank you for bringing this young man to my attention." They turned to see that the wayward soul had passed out on a nearby cot.

"He's actually a heroin addict and he would not have survived another night out there. He'll be having a rough day ahead as he goes through withdrawal symptoms. You did a good thing kids."

"Thanks Walt. And thank you for the work you do here. It is very important. There are a lot of people living in darkness and we need to help them into the light."

Walt was profoundly warmed by Mikaela's thoughtfulness. He could see she was special.

After getting their candy and then meeting their friends at the park to play, Mikaela and Zachary returned home. Mikaela rushed into her mother's room to find her asleep. She called out to her father and brother but there was no reply. Concerned she went down to the kitchen and made her mother a bowl of soup. She brought it up to her just as she was waking up.

"Mikaela, thank you sweetheart for making me soup."

Zachary was in tow with a plate of bread and butter.

"You guys didn't have to do that. Where's your father?"

"I'm not sure," Mikaela said, shrugging her shoulders.

"Do you feel any better mom?" asked a concerned Zachary.

"Still feel weak and tired."

It was hard for the children to see their once strong and vibrant mother so out of action. Mikaela propped up her mother's pillows so Jayne could sit up and have her soup. The children stayed with her for a couple of hours, catching her up on the day's events. When she had grown tired, the children took the plates downstairs.

After their grandmother arrived, they then both ran back upstairs, this time heading to the attic. When they walked into the attic they realized they had arrived too late to make another trip to heaven.

"Shoot, I was hoping we could go to heaven today," Mikaela said with sadness.

"Oh well, we can still play dragons and castles," Zachary said with delight. Mikaela smiled and agreed. She was starting to tire of children's games, but she could never refuse her little brother.

CHAPTER 11

Nightmares, Dreams and Reality

Later that night, after both Mikaela and Zachary had reluctantly gone to bed, Mikaela started to have a dream. She was dreaming about a large jet plane that was soaring through the air. It was flying through a beautiful bright blue sky with the sun beaming down on it. Later the sky started to turn to darkness. Then, with no explanation, the plane started to plummet to Earth. Mikaela realized she was on the ground looking up at the plane. She could see the plane coming down from a great distance on the horizon. She soon could hear the screaming sound of the engines as it came hurtling down. Mikaela began to look for a place to hide and started running to a nearby house. She would periodically look up and see that the plane was getting closer and closer. She ran through the front door of the house and went down to the basement as quickly as possible. Crouching down on the basement floor, she waited for the impact. She was so frightened and her heart was pounding in her chest. She waited and waited to hear the sound of an explosion, but it never came. She wondered what had happened. Had the plane somehow corrected itself? Maybe the pilots had regained control? She slowly walked upstairs and waited again in the living room. Still no explosion. She then walked outside to the porch and the looked up in the air. The sky was now dark. What had happened to the plane? She then walked around the side of the house. Off in the distance, miles away, the entire horizon seemed to be ablaze. It was like she had been punched in the stomach. She fell to her knees and started to weep uncontrollably. Just then her father woke her up.

"Mickey, Mickey, wake-up!"

"Oh dad, I just had the worst dream," she yelled as she grabbed him and pulled him to her. Charlie wrapped his arms around her and did his best to comfort her. She was shaking uncontrollably.

"What is it honey? That must have been a terrible dream."

"It was, it was!!! It was an airplane that crashed into the ground. All those poor people."

Mikaela eventually settled down and her dad continued to lay with her, stroking her head, trying to reassure her. As she calmed down and began to relax, she noticed it was four in the morning. Her father was still wearing his clothes from the previous day and not his pajamas.

"Why are you still in your regular clothes dad?"

"Ah, well, I've been up late, working on some ideas for work."

Mikaela looked into her father's eyes. She could tell he was not telling the truth.

"Dad, what's going on really?"

"Nothing for you to worry about dear, now go back to sleep."

Charlie gave her a kiss on the head and then headed for the master bedroom. Mikaela, still trembling from her dream, slowly got back to sleep.

Downstairs in the basement, Jake was lying on the cot with Stella. They had just finished a passionate kiss and both wondered where it would go next. Breaking the tension, Jake jumped out of bed and went to the doorway where he pulled out his guitar. Stella smiled and sat up. Jake started playing a few chords and began to sing. The song which he had been working on for a few weeks was a bit simple. The lyrics were a little dramatic at times with him pledging his allegiance;

*Our relationship has caused commotion but
I will always give you my devotion.*

And its poetic chorus was a little on the rough side:

*Stella, I want to be your fella
Love you, is what I want to tell'ya*

The song had a total of three chords but Stella seemed please, as she applauded her troubled troubadour.

"So what'dya think?"

"I thought it was cute."

"Cute? It's a masterpiece!"

"I especially liked the presentation. Not many men can pull off a serenade in their jammies."

"Hey these are men's boxers I'll have you know."

Jake gave Stella a loving smile. He then quickly ditched the guitar and hopped back onto bed.

"Jake, do you love me?"

"Of course I do. Do you think I'd risk my neck by having you live in the basement? If my parents had any idea I would be dead."

"Well to that point, if you really love me, why don't you find us a place to live?"

"A place to live? How would we afford that?"

"Well, I'm graduating next year. I could get a job. You could get a job."

"Well, I'm just trying to get through high school and I would really like to go to college."

"Really, with your grades?"

"How do you know what my grades are?"

Stella thought for a moment, "You told me a while back."

"Really?" Jake began to think. He never remembered discussing his grades with her but maybe she was right.

"Anyway, in the meantime, I think there are many other ways you can prove your love to me."

"Like what?"

"I need a tablet."

"A tablet. Those things cost a fortune."

"Well, if you really love me, you'll get me one."

Now Jake's love for Stella was really on the line. Did he love her enough to steal for her? The last time he tried to steal something he almost got himself shot and might be responsible for someone dying. According to Mikaela however he wasn't. But how did Mikaela know that? He again question his sister's truthfulness.

"Also, I want a formal dinner date. I want you to take me out to a nice restaurant; a nice dinner, flowers, dancing, the whole nine yards as they say."

Jake's forehead became furrowed thinking how he would pull of these requests. She patted him on the shoulder and gave him a loving wink of the eye. It gave Jake confidence. He was feeling more confident these days. If he was keeping his girlfriend happy he guessed he was doing something right. As long as she didn't complain he was happy, or at least somewhat happy. Having Stella in the basement was starting to wear on him. He felt a little depressed coming down to the "catacombs" as he now liked to refer to it. It looked cool and damp and dark. He was surprised that Stella could tolerate it for so long. She seemed to almost thrive in it. He knew she would leave for a few hours at a time and occasionally for a day or two, but still, to be in this place for so long was a mystery to him. There were a lot of mysterious things about Stella. But he really enjoyed having a girl in his life. With all the stress of having to do well in school and his mother's illness, it was the one good thing in his life he could count on.

******

The next day, Mikaela played quietly in the backyard with Zachary. She was feeling a little unsettled by the nightmare she had the previous evening. She felt vulnerable, like maybe something bad was about to happen. Was her mother going to die? Was something bad going to happen to her father or brothers? She felt like life was becoming a little out of control. She did not like things being out of control. She liked organization and having control over everything in her life. Maybe Mother Light was trying to teach her something? Maybe she could talk to Mother Light later that day? She hoped that the rain that was forecast would not come. She wanted to visit heaven again.

Later in the day, all her friends from her party came over. They played soccer all afternoon until the rain came. At that point they all went up to the attic to play. Before they went to the attic they all went into Jayne's room to pay a visit and to see if she needed anything.

"Hello girls. It's so nice to see you all."

"Hello Mrs. Royalton. How are you feeling?" Becky asked.

"Oh, a little better, I'm planning to get up in a little bit and take a walk around the house."

"Maybe dad can help you?"

"Yes, where is your father?"

"I saw him in the garage earlier. He's building a work bench and adding some new drywall."

"Oh that's good, maybe he'll have time to walk with me."

"I guess those treatments are not helping Mrs. Royalton?" the ever blunt and obnoxious Brittany asked.

"Brittany!" Mattie yelled.

"No that's okay. It's good to ask questions Brittany. You don't learn anything by not asking questions."

Brittany gave Mattie a sneer.

"Yes, it is helping Brittany. I'm just adjusting to a new diet that the doctor has put me on but I am hopeful the treatments will help."

"Is it chemo?" the inquisitive Brittany asked.

"It's a combination of chemo and a new hormone therapy. The cancer was aggressive at first and so we were using chemo but we are hoping that we can just move to a hormone therapy only."

Brittany smiled as if all her questions had been satisfactorily answered. Jayne smiled at her knowing that while she might be abrasive to others, she appreciated Brittany's honest questions.

The girls all went into the attic and began to play. With the exception of Mikaela they enjoyed listening to the rain pelt the window. It soon turned into a thunderstorm with lightning and thunder.

The girls stood looking out at the backyard as the rain poured down.

"Wow, I feel like I'm on a ship in the middle of a storm," Greta said in an excited voice.

"Yeah, let's play pirates!" Becky asked

"No, not pirates," Mikaela said.

"Why not Mickey? Ya gonna get all weird on us again about what women are supposed to do?" Brittany said with scorn.

At that moment, the rain stopped and the sun started to beam through an opening in the clouds.

"Wow, that is so cool!" Mattie yelled. The girls turned back to the window and looked at the heavenly lights. Mikaela looked up to the ceiling windows and hoped the lights would start beaming down on them. It was late enough in the day where direct sunlight would be able to shine into the ceiling windows. She hoped and prayed that it would. As the girls continued to be awed by the light, Mikaela could see little flickers coming down through the ceiling windows. She watched as it slowly turned into a long beam of light and then began to shine on the back wall of the attic. Slowly the portal began to appear. Becky, who had already experienced heaven was looking too.

"Where's Zachary?" Greta asked, also knowing what was about to happen.

"Oh, he's in the garage helping my dad." The pair who were normally joined at the hip were experiencing their first separation from each other. Her father feeling it might be more "healthy" if Zachary started spending more time with him. Mikaela just hoped that whatever her father was going through wouldn't impact Zachary.

As Brittany and Mattie continued to talk, Mikaela, Marnie, Lola, Becky and Greta walked toward the back wall. As the light began to shine directly on the wall, they could see something almost like sparks or when someone lights a sparkler during firework celebrations. As these little fits and sparks of light happened, the outline of the door slowly appeared.

"Wow!" Becky yelled.

Brittany and Mattie both turned to see what was happening. Both had a look of horror on their faces.

"What in the world?" Brittany exclaimed.

"What is that?!!!" Mattie said gasping.

"C'mon," Mikaela waved for them to come over. As they did so Greta put her arm around Mattie to reassure her while Mikaela did the same to Brittany. All seven girls then walked up to the door. Mikaela without hesitation pulled on the rope and the door was open.

"What is this place?" Brittany asked trembling.

"It's a doorway to heaven. C'mon. Don't be afraid!"

Both Greta and Mikaela practically pushed Mattie and Brittany through the door. Lola and Marni hesitantly followed. As the uninitiated girls slowly stepped into the field, they fully expected to fall into Mikaela's backyard. When they realized they were on firm ground they could not believe their eyes.

"C'mon, let's run!!!" Greta yelled.

The girls began to run as fast as they could, Mattie and Brittany realized they were running faster than anyone could ever run on Earth. They were all soon airborne and zooming their way to-and-fro. Brittany, Mattie, Marnie and Lola began to scream with delight as the other three girls just smiled a knowing smile.

They soon arrived at the temple and everyone landed, Brittany though stumbled slightly. The orbs greeted Brittany, Mattie, Marnie and Lola for the first time and filled them in on where they had arrived. After the briefing, all the children enjoy the feast and then were joined by Mother Light. Mikaela introduced the new girls to Mother Light. While initially stunned at what they were seeing and doing, Brittany, Mattie, Marnie and Lola soon become quite comfortable with their surroundings. They had a feeling of warmth that Mikaela had experienced many times. It was a feeling of being home, of being in the real world. A world free from strife and turmoil. While

Brittany had come from a broken home, Mattie had secretly wrestled with ADHD and had always found it difficult to focus while in school. She had always felt inferior to the other girls but had a special bond with Mikaela. Mikaela, while not openly speaking about Mattie's learning concerns, had sensed certain things were difficult for her and would always give her extra attention, especially as it pertained to homework.

"Girls, I am so glad you were able to come today. Mikaela has spoken about you so often. I want to teach you some things today before you go back to Earth."

All the girls sat in rapt attention, all wanting to hear what Mother Light had to say.

"As you have probably learned from Mikaela, there is a darkness where you live on Earth. Not only the physical darkness but spiritual and moral darkness. Everything on Earth is a reflection of the reality here in heaven. You have a sun that brings you light, but it is a mere reflection of the true Great Light that brings light here in heaven. And not only does the Great Light bring physical light or a physical appearance, but it illuminates what is important; love. Love is the most important thing. To love yourself and to love others."

"Mother Light, what if someone hates you?" Brittany asked.

"When someone hates you, they are living in darkness. It is even more important to love those who hate you because they are truly in a dark place. We need to help everyone living in darkness to move to the light."

"Now, the most important thing we can do is love others, by helping them. We need to take the time to find out what is bothering someone. When we take that time we will find out what the issue is – they have usually been hurt by someone. We need to help them to overcome their hurt and move forward – forward into the light."

"Mother Light, Mikaela was telling us that the most important thing we can do as girls is to become mothers. Is that true?"

"Life is a reflection of love. Life is just as important as love. We must cherish life and therefore the most important thing for both men and women is to give life, to preserve life."

Mother Light could see that Brittany was mulling over her words.

"Now I can tell you are thinking about how fun it would be if you were the world's greatest soccer player. There is nothing wrong with that, but there are more important things for the people on Earth to focus on. Having a career is not wrong, but there are far greater things to do in life than be a lawyer, or a businessperson, or a soccer player.

Giving life and educating the young, there is nothing greater than that."

"What about being a doctor?"

"Yes, very important, especially if that doctor is promoting life and helping people to stay healthy. But there are doctors who do not do that. They act selfishly and live in the darkness. They think what they are doing is correct but it is not."

"Do I have to do what my husband says?" Brittany asked.

"It is important to be a team. Sometimes it is important to listen to your husband and sometimes it is important for a husband to listen to his wife. Many years ago, when human life had not existed for too long, men and women had to live off the land. It was the woman's job to be the nurturer; stay at home, take care of children and to keep the home. It was the man's job to go and hunt and forage for food. Both jobs are important. Unfortunately today, since the Earth has become a dark place, there are confused people. They will tell you that men just want to force women to be their subjects and in some cases that has been the truth. But the real truth is, men and women have separate roles, both completely equal to each other, but different. The people who live in darkness despise this truth."

Mikaela began to think about Principal Wilson and how she tried to silence Mikaela on her beliefs on family.

"What if someone doesn't agree with these ideas, like my principal?"

"Your principal, and many other people live in darkness so they cannot understand these things. These words are like gibberish to them. But you need to stand firm and stand up for what is good and right…show them the Great Light."

Finishing her lesson, Mother Light bid the children goodbye as they got ready to return to Earth. As they did so, Mikaela walked close to Mother Light.

"Mother Light, I had a terrible dream last night. It was about an airplane crashing. I've never heard or seen anything so terrible before in my life."

"Yes my child. Your mind is troubled. You feel like things are going out-of-control, with your mother, your brother and now your father. Please do not be alarmed. Stay strong. I will help you. The Great Light will help you. You need to trust us and believe. Now, as you grow older, you will become even more sensitive to the darkness on Earth. The things that mankind does will become more and more exposed to you. You will be sensitive to when someone is lying to you, when someone disrespects you…when someone means to do you harm. You are a strong girl Mikaela and do not lose hope."

"Will my mom be okay?"

"She may suffer in this present life, but yes, she will be okay. Keep helping her."

"And my brother and father?"

"They are both having clouded minds. They have both lost focus on what is important. You have to help them see the light."

"I will try my best Mother."

"I know you will."

Although she did not physically see Mother Light move toward her, Mikaela felt as though Mother Light was giving her a hug. A hug so tight and so warm she had never felt before. At that point, Mikaela smiled and motioned for the other girls to follow her. They ran through the columns of the temple and then launched themselves into the air. Flying had now become second nature to Brittany, Mattie, Marnie and Lola - having been given some tips from the orbs. As they zoomed into the open door of the attic, the girls came tumbling down onto the floor. They all burst into laughter and began to help each other get up.

"So what did you think Brittany?"

"Well either that was the greatest trick in history or we went to heaven."

"Well?"

"I can't believe we went to heaven!!!" she screamed with delight.

"When can we go again?" Mattie asked eagerly.

"I don't know. You can only go back when the sun strikes the windows just right and reveals the portal."

"Doesn't that happen every day?"

"No, sometimes there is rain. At different times of the year the sun is lower in the sky and does not appear directly in the window."

"Bummer."

"It is, but what I've learned from Mother Light is that we need to spend as much time on Earth as possible to help others."

The girls were all silent, thinking about Mikaela's words.

"Hey, maybe we should start a club or something?" Mattie asked in an excited voice.

"What kind of club?"

"A club that helps others. You know like the Red Cross or UNICEF."

"Those are not really clubs, they're organizations."

"Okay, whatever they are. We could create a club that helps others."

"So what would we do?"

"We could meet each week and talk about people that we have met who are in need. Then we could talk about how we can help them."

"That's a great idea Mattie. We can meet here every week in my attic."

"Hey what's going on?" Zachary yelled as he came into the room. "Did you guys go to heaven without me?!!!"

"Sorry bro but we did. Hey, you can join the new club we created."

Zachary didn't seem too convinced on the idea, but he typically relented when it came to anything his sister wanted him to do.

"What should we call it?"

"How about the KHP? Kids Helping People?"

"That's kinda lame," Brittany said in her usual acid tone. She quickly realized that she had used negative language and corrected herself.

"Sorry! It's good. Not great but good," she said, patting Becky on the shoulder for her suggestion.

"Okay, what day do we meet?"

"Well, we all have soccer practice on Tuesdays and Thursdays. How about Wednesdays?"

"That's good for me."

"Good for me too."

"Me too!"

Lola, Marnie and Becky nodded their heads.
"Sounds like Wednesday it is."

CHAPTER 12

The KHP (The Kids Helping People Club)

The next day when the girls returned to school, they all now had a new view on life, especially Brittany and Mattie who had just been to heaven for the first time. At lunch, several of the boys who played at the same club as the girls came over to their table.

"Why are you guys dressed that way?" one of the boys asked as he walked by.

"Dressed what way?"

"I don't know, but you look different.

All the girls had agreed to wear dresses that day to give a more feminine look to their group. They usually wore pants and jeans but decided they needed to not conform to what the world was telling them to.

"We are girls and girls wear dresses."

The boy pondered Mikaela's response and then smiled and walked to his table. From that point on the girls noticed the boys looking at them with a different look than they had seen before. They started to like the attention.

"What are you starring at Jeffery Scott?" Mikaela yelled across the cafeteria. Jeff Scott immediately looked the other way not wanting to invite the wrath of Mikaela.

The commotion in the cafeteria caught the ear of Principal Wilson who walked in and began to look around. The girls immediately turned toward each other and without saying a word decided they better keep it down. The principal walked by their table.

"Hello children. Everything okay?"

"Yes Ms. Wilson."

"Please call me Principal Wilson Mikaela."

"Yes, sorry Principal Wilson."

The principal continued to stare at the girls. They seemed different to her and she did not like it. She did not like when children tried to stand out from the others. Like many on Earth, she was living in the dark. She eventually relented and walked away. The girls let out a sigh of relief and then began to nervously giggle.

******

On the way home from school, Mikaela was walking with Zachary. They took a different route home to see if they could find any new adventures for Zachary. While Zachary swung his imaginary sword which was just a large stick he had found in an abandoned lot, Mikaela saw a young girl walking down the street. What caught Mikaela's attention was that the girl seemed very pre-occupied and alone. As they walked up behind the girl, Mikaela could see she was probably an older teen.

As they neared the girl, the sun started shinning down on them and Mikaela could feel a sudden surge of warmth and strength. She felt like she did when she was embraced by Mother Light. As she looked at the young girl in front of her she could see she had a darkness over her. She was pregnant and becoming desperate.

Oh where is this place? God, I need to find it soon. Dammit, where is it?!!!

Not sure if she was hearing the young teen out loud, Mikaela could clearly hear her thoughts. She looked over to Zachary to see if he was hearing the same thing but he was busy waving his stick around. As they continued walking, Mikaela could sense that the young teen was looking for an abortion clinic. As they neared a building at the edge of town, it looked gray and dark. The sun had stopped shinning and was behind some dark clouds.

"Hello, miss!"

The young teen shuddered as Mikaela called out to her. She turned around. She had the look of profound fear in her eyes.

"Can I help you?"

"Help me. You're just a kid, leave me alone."

"Please, don't go in that building."

"Why?"

"Because inside that building is nothing but darkness and death. Please do not go in."

When Mikaela said that, she captured Zachary's full attention and he slowly dropped his stick to the ground.

"Who are you guys?"

"My name is Mikaela and this is my brother Zachary."

"Okay and so what do you want?"

"We just want you to think about what you are doing. I know this is really difficult but killing your unborn child is not the solution."

"So, are you going to take care of it?"

"It's not an it…it's a boy or a girl, it's a living human being."

"How old are you?"

"I'm eleven."

"You're eleven, so what do you know about it?"

"I know to take a human life is not right."

"So are you going to help me raise he or she then?"

Mikaela stopped to think about it. She knew they had plenty of room at their house.

"Look, why don't you come home with us and we can discuss it with my parents."

The girl sighed and looked at Mikaela. She could see that Mikaela was serious. She then looked at the decrepit building that looked dark and grimy. As they continued to look at the building two other young teens approached from the other direction. One was crying and the other who looked to be her friend was consoling her. They opened the door and walked in.

"Look, if you go in there like those two, you'll never be able to forgive yourself. Human life is the most precious thing in the world."

"Yeah, but I don't want to be a mother. I want to go to school and have a career."

"So, you didn't think about that when you were having sex?"

The young teen began to look at Mikaela. It was one thing to be lectured by her parents or another adult, but this was an eleven-year-old. Why in the world was she so concerned for a stranger's behavior?

"Look, I appreciate your concern, but this is my body, it's my life, not yours!"

"Yes, but you are taking someone's life…you will be killing another human being. If you are so concerned about having a career, why didn't you think about that before having sex? You're destroying someone else for your own selfishness."

The girl shook her head and then began to walk toward the clinic.

"Please think about it!!!" Mikaela and Zachary watched as the young teen walked into the clinic. Mikaela turned to Zachary with a look of utter sadness and helplessness.

"C'mon Zachary, let's go home."

"Should we go in there and try and talk to her?" Zachary asked. Mikaela shook her head and motioned for him to walk with her.

"This is the reason why people should listen to us kids. Clearly adults have no clue what's going on to allow this to happen."

"Yeah, they're really dumb."

Mikaela put her arm on her brother's shoulder and they began to walk home.

Across town, Jake was walking by an electronics store. He walked around to the back to look at the loading dock. Looking up at the sky, he could see it was getting dark and that it would be raining soon. In the back there was a delivery truck that was backed into the loading dock. He slowly walked around to where the truck was and began to peer inside the back of the store. He could not hear or see anyone. He then looked into the back of the delivery truck. There were all kinds of boxes loaded. He then climbed the stairs that were to the side of the loading dock and quickly ran into the truck. He grabbed a box and then hopped down to the ground, placed it into his backpack and began to run as fast as he could.

As Jake ran around to the front, he stopped and hid behind a wall. He looked back to make sure no one had seen him. He then started to walk down the sidewalk, acting like he had done it a thousand times before. To some extent he had, at least in his mind. He had been planning the heist for a while. Every day he had walked down to the electronics shop after school and began to observe the comings and goings of everyone to the shop. They had deliveries on Tuesdays and Thursdays, always at the same time. He timed the movements of the driver. It always took him about 10 minutes to walk to the front of the store to have the manager sign-off on the delivery, just enough time for Jake to pull off the theft.

As Jake walked down the street, he was pleased with himself. It took a lot of ingenuity. But as he walked further, he began to feel a sense of wrongdoing. *Maybe I should take it back?* He began to think of Stella however and the thought quickly passed.

As he arrived home he called out to the rest of the family but there was no response. He ran upstairs to check on his mother but she was sound asleep. His grandmother was sitting in a rocking chair next to his mother and motioned for him to keep his voice down. He could hear his brother and sister up in the attic but decided not to bother them. He then ran back downstairs and down to the basement. Arriving at the backroom, he knocked gently and then was granted entry by the sultry Stella. She was wearing only a black bra and panties; both flowery and very shear. He took the box out of his backpack and handed it to her.

"Oh my love, you got it, a tablet! Come here you rascal," she said as she pulled him onto the cot. The couple engaged in a long round of kissing and one of the most passionate Jake estimated. Being a "bad boy" as Stella was now calling him, made the session seem even more erotic and sensual. As the two lay in bed, Stella reminded Jake of her other request.

"So that was request one, you now have to take me out for a fancy dinner somewhere."

"Anywhere in particular?"

"I'll let you decide. You are taking me out on a date. It's your job as the man to decide."

As the "man." Jake had never been called a man before. He liked the sound of that. He felt like he was an adult. He loved the way Stella made him feel. He would do anything for her and his conscience was numb to whether that "anything" was right or wrong. He had slowly slipped into a moral darkness and while still young and able to be rehabilitated, he was playing in a dangerous arena.

When Jake went back upstairs to get something to eat, he was met by Mikaela.

"Hey Jake, how are you doing?"

"Okay, how about you?" he said with a look of contentment she never remembered him ever having.

"Jake, please be careful. You are hanging around some bad people."

"What are you talking about?"

"I know things. I know that you have been with some boys who have gotten into trouble. You also got into some trouble with them."

"Look Mikaela, I have no idea of what you are talking about."

"Mr. Harris?"

"What about him?"

"Remember what I told you?"

"About Mr. Harris? You said I bet he forgives you or something like that."

"No. I actually talked with Mr. Harris. He told me directly that he forgives you."

Jake took out some bread and a container of salami and then slowly closed the refrigerator door. As he did so, Mikaela was looking at him with a very serious look.

"Mikaela. I think there is something terribly wrong with you if you believe you actually spoke to a dead man."

"He is not dead. He's in heaven."

"You're kidding me. That old grump is in heaven? They must let anybody in."

"He is actually a good man. He did forget about the most important thing in life was that he needed to help people, and as he grew older he put that aside, but it didn't change the fact that he was a person of love and light."

"You sound crazy right now. Leave me alone."

"I also know you are in a relationship that is not good for you…with a girl."

"You know about Stella?"

"I don't know the specifics, but it was revealed to me that you are with someone that can do you harm."

"Hi kids, how's your mom?"

Charlie walked through the kitchen door interrupting Mikaela and Jake's conversation.

"Hi dad. She just woke up and is hungry. I was getting her a snack. She's with Nanna now."

"Thanks Mickey. And how are you young man?"

"I'm fine. Hey, can I use the SUV Friday night?"

"What's wrong with your car?"

"Ah, it just doesn't look good for a date."

"Sure, that's fine. Good luck on your date!"

With that Jake left the kitchen leaving Mikaela and her father alone.

"So how have you been Mickey?"

"Fine."

"Just fine?"

"Well, I do wonder where you go to. You seem to not be around much these days?'

Charlie was taken aback. He had not noticed himself how much he had been gone.

"Well, I've been working on a project. If the project is successful for the company it will mean new business with the city and then more revenue. More revenue for the company then more income for our family."

"Is more money that important? Isn't it more important to spend time with us, with mom?"

"Yes it is, but without your mom's income it is difficult to afford all the things we are used to."

"What things?"

"Ah well, all the TV shows everyone wants to watch. The gas bill, the water bill, the electric bill. We are a family of high consumption."

"Maybe we can stop using so much. Can we help?"

"Honey, the only thing you need to worry about is school and having fun. Life is short and you need to enjoy your childhood."

"Dad, life in this world is short but the world to come is for eternity."

Charlie stopped to look at his daughter. She had a very convinced look on her face. He had always known that his daughter was very focused and very intelligent, but now she seemed to have a glow of wisdom about her. Did she know about all the things he had been up to? He gave her a smile and nodded.

"Perhaps you're right dear, perhaps you're right. Now, why don't you run this snack up to mom? I'll be up there in a minute."

As Mikaela left the kitchen, Charlie walked over to his den. He went over to his work desk where he picked up a picture. It was a picture of the entire family on a vacation they had taken to Florida. They all looked so happy and healthy in the photograph. He missed those days. At the moment he was feeling very alone and depressed.

After giving her mother her snack, Mikaela helped her get dressed. It was a struggle but they were able to put on an old track suit Jayne had kept from her high school days. Mikaela then helped her with her tennis shoes and with the aid of her grandmother and Zachary, raised Jayne to her feet. She very slowly regained her balance as she began to move. With each step she was getting stronger and stronger, or so they hoped. She did seem more energetic than normal so the children were optimistic.

"How you feeling dear?" Charlie asked as he came to the bedroom door.

"A little better."

"Hey kids and Nanna, I'll help your mom."

Charlie then helped Jayne downstairs and then out to the front porch where she took a quick breather. Mikaela and Zachary watched from their upstairs bedroom as their father helped their mother to walk down the street. Jayne looked like she was regaining some of her strength as her pace began to quicken. Mikaela smiled. Maybe this would also help their parents to reconnect again.

"How have things been going at work?" Jayne asked.

"Good. I have a project with the city that looks like it's going to happen."

"Oh, that's good. I haven't seen you around much lately."

Charlie was silent as he continued to hold her up by the shoulder. She stopped and then turned toward him to look him in the face. She smiled and then studied his eyes. She could see he was troubled.

"Yes, I guess I've been spending a little too much time at the office. I think Becky's mom has been coming over though?" Charlie then took Jayne by the hand and they again began to walk.

"Yes, she's been a big help. But I really miss you. Even when you're at home, it seems, well, like you're not at home. You're somewhere else."

"I guess it's the business."

"Do you still love me?"

Charlie stopped in his tracks and then looked up to the sky. He turned and pulled Jayne close to him, looking her in the eyes.

"Of course I do."

"I'm no longer the woman you married. I feel gross most of the time, little time to give to you."

"Please don't worry about me. Just worry about getting healthy. Hopefully, one day, we will all be back to normal."

"What if we're not?"

Charlie motioned for Jayne to keep walking. He pulled her by the hand and she reluctantly complied.

"Remember what the doctor said during our last appointment? You're looking a lot better, your white blood cell count is down, and you passed all your other tests. It's just about getting stronger now and keeping up your treatments. Your body has been in a state of atrophy. You need to strengthen your muscles."

Jayne studied her husband. She knew he had been under a lot of duress during her illness, but was there something else bothering him? He typically bottled things inside, not being open about a lot of what was happening to him. He just seemed even more secretive as of late. They continued the rest of their walk mostly in silence.

CHAPTER 13

A Dark Affair

Charlie Royalton had worked for McCaskey and Lund for over 12 years. He was now a Senior Project Manager for the company and not only did that mean a bump in salary, but he was also now up for bonuses. The new project he was leading was a bid for a new environmental center right near where the Royaltons lived. Part of the reason why the Royaltons had purchased the house on Arendelle Court was because it backed onto a 5,000-acre nature reserve. The city now wanted to reclaim part of that marshland and forest to build a large park and environmental center. The fun part for Charlie was that he now needed to do some research on the area by his home. He needed to find out property boundaries and basically a history of what the area had been used for prior to the neighborhood being built.

Jessica "Jessie" Brewer was a newly employed engineer for McCaskey and Lund and had been assigned to Charlie's project. Over the past several months, Charlie and Jessie had grown close. Charlie took pride in mentoring young, up and coming engineers, and Jessie also happened to be a good listener. Jessie could often sense Charlie's moods and she would invite him to share what was going on in his life. They often went out to lunch together or grabbed a beer after work. It was therapeutic for Charlie in a number of ways.

The pair spent most of the day doing research on the proposed "Franklin Marsh Environmental Center." Charlie became fascinated with the information he found on the Arendelle Heights neighborhood they had moved to. Originally, in the early 1800's the town of Augsburg had been a mining town. The neighborhood just to the west was called Aunsbruck, which today is Arendelle Heights. Aunsbruck was a small neighborhood that supported the mining in Augsburg and was where the owner and several managers lived. In fact, the house where the Royaltons lived was once a small processing mill and had a large area below the current main basement. It had all been filled in to serve as a foundation for the new home.

Another surprising piece of history of the area was that the mines and mills were owned by the Krieg family. They had been immigrants from Germany in 1818 and had settled in the area. What was even more interesting is that they merged their business with Harrell and Sons in 1909. "Harrell?" Charlie deduced that Mrs. Harrell from down the street must have been a descendant.

"Hey Charlie, look at this," Jessie pointed to her computer. Charlie walked over and looked at a scan of an old newspaper article. The article was about a local artist. He had purchased what was now the Royalton's home. The article went on to talk about how the famous artist had purchased the home in 1926 from Jonathan Harrell. The artist Floyd Weatherby was known for his wild watercolors and had changed the attic into an art studio complete with ceiling windows so he would be able to get plenty of light while painting. Doing further internet searches they discovered that Weatherby had died in 1928 and the house went into probate. It was then purchased by Phillip Harrell. Phillip Harrell was the grandfather of Mrs. Eileen Harrell who now lived down the street. The house had been owned temporarily by Eileen but later sold because it had become too large. She moved into the smaller house down the street that she resides in today.

"This information is amazing. Oh, sorry Jessie. I've kept you here late. Looks like it's time to go. It's almost 9 o'clock."

"Oh, I'm fine. I can stay as long as you need me."

Charlie looked into Jessie's eyes. They were a light green and seemed translucent. She had an incredible smile and it melted Charlie's heart every time.

"Why don't we grab a drink? Let's celebrate our upcoming project."

"Well, it's not a done-deal yet."

She gave him a reassuring look to which he eventually gave in.

"Okay, let's grab a beer at Lenny's."

"Great, I'll grab my bag."

Charlie and Jessie headed out of the doors of McCaskey and Lund and walked a block down the street to Charlie's favorite tavern. He began to think of his wife. He knew that his mother-in-law was spending the night and would take care of her and the children. Besides, he had been working hard and was feeling the stress of the project. It was time to loosen up a bit. They walked into the Tavern and grabbed a table near the window. Charlie ordered a couple of beers from the waitress.

"Are you hungry?"

"No I am fine," Jessie replied.

"Can I get a brisket sandwich?"

The waitress smiled and nodded. It was late for a sandwich and Charlie knew he would regret it later but he was keeping a close eye on his weight. Jessie had been too. She had grown attracted to Charlie. Charlie was the kind of man that she had always imagined being with. He was smart, charming, funny and had a great career. His looks didn't hurt either. He was the whole package, or at least she thought so. She also knew that he was vulnerable. Not that she wanted to take advantage of that, but she wanted to at least be a shoulder to cry on or a good listener. And it was not that she wanted Jayne to pass away, but she thought that there might be an opportunity though if she did. She thought it a terrible idea though and quickly erased it from her mind.

"So how is Jayne doing?"

"Better. The new hormone therapy treatments seem to be working. She obviously had a step back with the minor stroke she had but she is getting her strength back."

"Oh that's good. Hopefully she'll make a full recovery."

Charlie thought of the ramifications of that as he stared into Jessie's beautiful eyes. Not that he didn't want Jayne to recover, but he was feeling a strong connection with Jessie. He quickly shook the thought of an affair from his mind. He questioned why he had offered to take Jessie to the tavern. Clearly he was inviting temptation. Jessie looked back at Charlie with a misty look in her eye. A look like she completely understood how he was feeling. Not only that he was suffering because of his wife, but because she knew that he wanted to be with her. Although a man, and somewhat oblivious to non-verbal clues, Charlie did pick-up on what she was communicating.

"So how are you doing, still living in the apartment down the street?"

"Yep. It's okay. It's close to everything so I am happy. The neighbors are a little weird but I think it's safe."

After several rounds of beers and a brisket sandwich, the couple decided to leave. The streets had grown quiet with only an occasional passerby. When they arrived at the apartment, an awkward silence began as they stopped in front of her front door.

"Would you like to come in?"

Charlie stood staring into her eyes. She knew he wanted to. She moved in closer to him. His mind was numb and it wasn't interested in obeying moral laws. He pulled her closer. He loved the feel of her as he clasped her hips. She was warm and sensual. They kissed. Charlie pulled back to look into her eyes. They were the same misty and inviting brilliant orbs. He then gave her a more passionate kiss which resulted in her quickly looking for the keys in her bag. She located them and she put the key into the lock. They practically broke the door down as she turned the key. Charlie began to laugh as he saw how they almost broke the doorknob off. He grabbed her again and they began to embrace. She stopped him for a moment and pointed to her bedroom. She grabbed him by the hand and pulled him into the bedroom. She then closed the door behind them.

After a heated sexual encounter, Charlie and Jessie lay panting on their backs, both staring at the ceiling, the inevitable regret started settling in for Charlie. He didn't look at Jessie. What was he to do? Should he tell Jessie it had been a big mistake? Should he tell Jayne? Would God forgive him? While not an overtly religious person, he did feel the concept of good and evil and that there was a moral code. He had definitely transgressed that code.

Charlie eventually looked over at Jessie who was still entranced by the molding on the ceiling. He could tell she was also feeling regret. Jessie, while feeling close to Charlie and who had been feeling lonely, now felt she had betrayed another woman. She had never wanted to do that but in a moment, maybe a month of building passion, had given in. Charlie in silence got out of bed and quietly put his clothes on. He tried to think of something to tell Jessie but they were both feeling a strong sense of betrayal. How would they get passed this? They were working on a project together. It wasn't like they could easily slip into another project, another role, another department.

As Charlie finished dressing, he took another look at Jessie. She had turned on her side facing away from him with the covers over her. He slowly and quietly slipped out of the apartment. He walked back to the office parking structure where he got into his truck and drove home. It was a quiet, dark and guilt-ridden drive home.

As Charlie walked into the front door, he was startled to see Mikaela sitting on the couch, with the lights on in the living room. He walked over to her assuming she might be reading and had fallen asleep. Under closer inspection he could see she was awake and looking at him.

"Honey, what are you doing up?"

"Hi dad. I couldn't sleep."

"What's the matter?" Charlie joined Mikaela on the couch.

"I'm worried about you."

"Worried? Why?"

"Look dad, I know you're lonely, but what you are doing is not right. You need to stop. I know it's difficult but you need to think about mom…think about the family."

Charlie was dumbfounded. Was she talking about him working too much or about the affair he had just had? He looked at her and it felt like she was looking into his soul. He sat back and blew a stream of air from his mouth.

"Look honey, I know I have been working too late…"

"It's not that. It's the woman at work you are having a relationship with."

Charlie crinkled his forehead wondering how in the world Mikaela could know about it.

"What are you talking about?"

"Dad, I know things. When people sneak around in the dark, they do dark things. You are lost right now. I understand why. Mom is sick and we kids are always running around so you don't get any love and attention. But looking for love outside of the house is not good."

Charlie looked at Mikaela with a pale expression. How could his eleven-year-old daughter know he had had an affair? It had just happened so there was no way anyone could have told her. Was the sense of guilt he felt so evident on his face?

"How do you know whether I was with another woman?"

"Mother Light told me."

"Mother Light? Who is Mother Light?"

"She's this incredible lady who I met from this fantastic place."

"Where is this fantastic place?"

"Heaven."

Charlie was mortified. How could his daughter think she had been to heaven? Now he began to think about the conference he had with Mikaela's principal. Maybe she was having issues dealing with reality. Should he take her to a doctor?

"Look honey, I don't know who this lady is but you have to know that she isn't real."

"Oh she's real alright. The thing you need to know dad is that this world is not real. This world is fake. It's only a mere replica of heaven. We all need to focus on the light and getting to heaven. If we get too locked up in worldly pleasures and problems, we'll get weighed down by the dark and will never be able to see the light."

Charlie nodded his head and then began to look at the wall by the fireplace. There was a family portrait hanging over the fireplace. It was of a much happier time. A less stressful time.

"Okay honey, I think it is time for you to go to bed."

"Okay, but please listen to me dad. The only way I could have known about that woman is if it had been revealed to me. And also, you need to talk with Jake. He is involved with some of the same kind of things."

"Jake?"

"Yes, he's fooling around with drugs and sex."

Charlie was again horrified by Mikaela's revelation. She smiled with a look of sympathy and then turned around and walked upstairs. How could she know these things? He kept raking his brain but it seemed impossible for a young girl to know about the intimate details of other family members. He shook his head, got up and turned out the light in the living room. He slowly walked upstairs in the dark, worried about his next encounter with Jayne.

Charlie stumbled into their bedroom not wanting to awake Jayne. He took his clothes off as best as he could, leaving only his boxers on. He was too tired to search for his pajamas. He got into bed as gently as he could and began to stare at the ceiling. His head was spinning slightly and he watched as the ceiling fan went in and out of focus.

"Did you have a nice evening?" Jayne's voice surprised him. Lately, with her treatments, she had been sleeping soundly at night.

"Ah, yes, I did."

"Did you have a nice dinner?"

"Why do you ask?"

"I can smell the beer on your breath."

Charlie wanted to slap himself in the head for not brushing his teeth.

"Yeah, I went to Lenny's."

"By yourself?"

Charlie turned to look at Jayne. She was on her back staring at the ceiling. He could see she was wide awake. He turned over and switched the light on that was on his nightstand. The light was bright and he had to refocus. The light seemed brighter than usual. He turned back over and then sat up in bed with his back against the headboard. Jayne then also sat up in bed in a similar fashion. Charlie turned to look at her.

"Babe, I'm sorry. I need to tell you something."

"I'm listening."

"There's a girl at work," Charlie paused searching for words that might make what he was about to say seem better but he knew it would be impossible.

"Yes."

"Anyway, this girl at work and I have been working together on this new project," a lump began to form in Charlie's throat. How was he going to be able to speak? How was he going to tell the girl he married, his high school sweetheart, that he had betrayed her? Charlie and Jayne had known each other since they were both sixteen. Since that time Charlie had never even looked at another girl.

"Does this girl have a name?"

"Jessie," Charlie looked away from Jayne. Jayne nodded to herself knowing what had happened. Charlie looked back at Jayne and knew that she understood completely what had happened. He didn't even need to say the words. Perhaps Jayne was having mercy on him for not making him say it out loud.

"Will this happen again?"

"No. No! I realize how stupid I was. I'm sorry and I want things to go back as before."

Charlie moved closer to Jayne in an attempt to hug her. She looked deeply into his eyes.

"You've hurt me Charlie. And of all times now, you have really hurt me."

"I know, I know, is there anything I can do to fix this?"

Jayne sat and thought for a long time. Charlie stared at her praying for her forgiveness.

"Well, I suppose you were honest with me about it. If it happens again though, I…I'll take the kids and leave."

"Understood." Charlie turned away and began to nod his head. He nodded in an attempt to tell himself he would never do it again. Jayne turned over on her side facing away from Charlie. Charlie knew he had broken a sacred trust and bond and things between he and Jayne would never be the same again. He knew he would probably have to spend the rest of his life making it up to her.

As he lay awake that night, he had come to realize that he had received the courage to tell Jayne because of the feeling he had from Mikaela. It was a sense of duty, a sense of rightness that he needed to tell Jayne and that had come from Mikaela.

******

As Jake left the school grounds on his way home, he noticed a group of girls congregating near the main parking lot. From a distance, one of the girls looked like Stella. Why would she be hanging out with kids from a school she didn't attend? His mind began running in a million directions, trying to figure out a reason why she might be there. He walked to a nearby tree where he pretended to look around in his backpack. After a while two of the top "jocks" in school, joined the girls. Timmy Stevens was the All-American quarterback who all the girls daydreamed about. Timmy had been offered a full ride to play football the following year at the university. To say he was a stud was an understatement. Jake soon realized he was chatting up Stella and the two soon peeled off from the rest of the group and began to walk away from the school. Jake followed in hot pursuit, but keeping far enough away so he wouldn't be noticed.

As Stella and Timmy walked down the street, they neared the electronics shop that Jake had stolen the tablet from. He noticed the owner of the store in back talking to an employee. An immense sense of guilt filled him thinking about his theft. The feeling quickly subsided however when he saw that the football player was flirting with his girlfriend. As they reached the beginning of their neighborhood. The pair chatted a little while longer before she gave him a broad smile and nodded in affirmation of something. She said goodbye and began to walk down the cul-de-sac of Arendelle Court. Before she reached the Royalton's home, she quickly walked up the stairs of a house he wasn't familiar with. She seemed to know the place as she just walked in. He knew that Stella, especially as of late, was spending less and less time at his house. Perhaps she had found other places to stay in the neighborhood? Was he losing his bond with her? What could he do to not lose her? He had given her the tablet. He knew now he had to really win her back and go do the things she asked for like go on a fancy date to a restaurant. But where would he get the money for an expensive restaurant? He would have to steal it. But from where? His parents never had money around. Maybe the Harris place? Now that Mr. Harris was dead, maybe the only one left was Mrs. Harris? It seemed almost like sacrilege to go back there. Who knew, maybe Mrs. Harris was more ornery than Mr. Harris.

Jake walked into the cul-de-sac and slowed as he passed the house Stella had walked into. He tried to remember anything about the house. He seemed to recall Mikaela telling their father that a rather grumpy old lady lived there. Maybe it was the same lady who had broken up his and Stella's July 4th tryst? He tried to see inside but everything was in darkness. He pretended he had no interest in who lived there and then marched quickly to his house. Later that night he snuck down to the basement but Stella was not there.

The next morning, Mikaela went into her mother's room and found her sleeping. She could hear her father downstairs making breakfast. It made her happy. As she looked at her mother, she noticed her surroundings were quite dark. She walked over to the window and opened the curtains.

"What are you doing?" a rather groggy Jayne asked.

"Mom, you need light."

"I need to sleep my love."

"No you don't. You need exercise and you need light. The light will heal you."

Jayne lifted herself up and smiled at Mikaela. She motioned for Mikaela to come to her and give her a hug. As she did, Zachary came running into the room and plunged himself into the bed creating a shockwave.

"Good morning you little rascal," Jayne said as she pulled Zachary into a group hug.

"C'mon mom, you remember what the doctor said, 'you need to eat right and do exercise,'" Mikaela said in a deep voice trying to emulate the doctor. Jayne smiled and nodded her head. Both Mikaela and Zachary pulled her out of bed and then handed Jayne her robe. The trio then walked together downstairs where they greeted Charlie.

"Good mornin'!" Charlie said with a confident smile no one had remembered seeing in quite a while.

"I made pancakes."

The children cheered knowing they were getting their father's famous blueberry oatmeal pancakes with hot maple syrup. As the family congregated around the table, Mikaela looked toward the front entryway where she could see Jake. Jake was looking at her and motioning to her to come over to him. She walked over and could see him waving to her to come with him toward the front living room window.

"Hey, do you know whose house that is?'

"Yeah, that's Mrs. Harrell's house. Why?"

"No reason, I was just walking by there the other day and…I was just interested in who lived there."

"Well, she's a very grumpy old lady and I would not recommend getting on her bad side."

As Mikaela walked back into the kitchen, Jake began to make a plan. He would try and break into the house and see if Stella was still there as well as steal whatever goods or money he could find.

"Hey Jake, do you want to join us at the zoo today? We're going to get your mom some needed exercise. What do you say?"

"Thanks dad but I need to do some homework."

Mikaela smiled at Jake. Jake could see the look in Mikaela's eyes told him that she knew he was up to something.

******

After breakfast, the family headed to the zoo sans Jake. It turned out to be a wonderful day. It was bright and sunny, not too cold and not too warm, just perfect. The children were in pseudo-heaven because they felt as if they were a family again. Charlie and Jayne walked hand-in-hand and it was clear that Jayne was starting to regain some of her former self.

As they sat and ate lunch at one of the picnic tables, Charlie and Jayne began to talk. They looked into each other's eyes again with love and understanding. Mikaela could see they were connecting again.

"It's good to see you getting back to your old self."

"It's good to see you getting back to your old self," she said back with a wink.

"I'm sorry I haven't been there for you and the kids the past couple of months."

"I understand," Jayne said as she cupped his hands in hers.

"I was feeling sorry for myself and that was wrong," Jayne nodded in agreement.

As the children could see their parents becoming a little "mushy" they went over and played on a jungle gym.

"I know you've been under a lot of pressure since I stopped working but maybe that will all change. Tell me about the project you've been working on."

"It's actually pretty neat. We are building an environmental center by Franklin Marsh, just east of the house. I'm learning a lot about the area, especially during the colonial, industrial ages. Do you know our house was once actually a coal processing plant? There's a whole large basement that was used to house coal processing. There was a mine down below the house and coal was brought up on a conveyor belt to the processing mill that was right under our basement. It was since filled in when it was converted to a house."

"Wow, that's incredible. You never know what all has happened to the places around here, that's amazing."

"What's even more amazing is that Mrs. Harrell's family used to live there or her ascendants anyway."

"Really. Why does she live down the street then?"

"She used to live in our house but then when her parents died and her brothers and sisters moved away, she decided she did not want to live there anymore, it was too big. Did I tell you what happened during Mikaela's birthday party?" Jayne shook her head.

"She came over to the house complaining about the music. She was moving around like she owned the place."

"Well, she's older and alone, we have to respect her."

"Yeah, I guess. She's a bit surly though."

Jayne smiled. She enjoyed connecting with Charlie again. It had been a long time. She also understood Charlie's need to connect physically with someone and she hoped she could one day fulfill that need. He was a good man.

While Charlie and Jayne were reconnecting, Mikaela and Zachary talked about what they had seen earlier.

"What about that poor little mouse being fed to the snake?" Zachary said with disgust. The children had witness one of the staff at the zoo, place a live mouse in one of the python enclosures.

"I know that was so sad."

"It makes me think that I want to be a vegetarian. Why do you suppose we have to eat meat? Doesn't it seem awful that animals have to die? Why would the Great Light make things this way?"

"I don't think that was the Great Light's intention. It was when humans decided they didn't want to live in the light anymore. When the Great Light created our new dimension, it was without true light. When there is no true light, everything becomes corrupted."

"Wow, you know everything Mickey!" Zachary said with pride.

"Mother Light told me. And deep down you know too. Everything is not how it should really be. We were given paradise but now we have darkness; disease, abuse, animals eating animals."

"Should we become vegetarians then?"

"Maybe. Right now let's focus on getting mom better."

"Maybe that will make her better if we take meat out of her diet?"

"Maybe." Mikaela smiled.

The rest of the day the family had a great time walking around the zoo. They finally tired and headed home. It had been a good day. They were a family again.

CHAPTER 14

Another Harrowing Heist

Later that night, Jake slipped down to the basement. Stella was again missing. He was starting to become angry and jealous. *Why didn't she want to live in the basement anymore?* As he said that to himself he realized what a dumb question it was. This wasn't the Ritz Carlton. While in the basement, he grabbed a canvas bag and a crowbar and flashlight as well as a ski mask. He then headed back upstairs. He noted the time was two o'clock in the morning. Hopefully this would be a good time to commit a burglary.

Jake went to the backyard and began to walk into the nearby forest near the marsh. It was the area that he and Stella laid during the 4th of July fireworks. He remembered that night fondly, with the exception of Mrs. Harrell, who he was now focused on getting revenge. Thinking of Mrs. Harrell, Jake became more angry. That 4th of July encounter marked a time when he and Stella were at their closest – possibly about to have the most intimate encounter of their relationship. They were closer than he could imagine any two people could ever be. But then thanks to Mrs. Harrell, the couple had been split apart.

As Jake worked his way around the forest and marsh area he eventually arrived at Mrs. Harrell's house. The good thing about the neighborhood was that there was a good distance between houses and plenty of trees to stay hidden behind. He slowly snuck up to the house and noticed a storm door just like what they had at the Royalton home. There was a large lock on the door so he knew he would have to enter by some other way. He walked around to the back of the house toward what looked like a den with a bay window. The base of the house had a rock façade and he was able to grab onto the individual stones and pull himself up. In his bag he pulled out a crowbar and began to pry at the window. The metal frame of the window was old and rusted and he was easily able to pry it open, breaking the clasp. He pushed the window open and pulled the curtain to the side. It looked like a home office with a desk and computer on it. As he entered the room he pulled down the ski mask over his face.

Once inside he turned on his flashlight and began to peer around the office. There were several desks. Upon inspection, the desks were only filled with paperwork and bills. He then walked toward the door of the den. As he did so he heard a creak from the floor. He stopped to make sure he hadn't awoken anyone. After a minute, he stepped into the hallway and looked down either side. He started walking toward what appeared to be the master bedroom. The floor again creaked and he waited a moment. He then entered a bedroom on the right-hand side of the hallway. He had turned off his flashlight earlier so his eyes could adjust to the dark. He continued into the bedroom and looked around. There was enough light coming in that he could make out a bed, a desk, an armoire and a chest of drawers. He could see there was no one in the bed. He began to look through the drawers and in the top one found a jewelry box. He began to quickly put the rings, pearls and assorted other pieces into his bag. Next to the jewelry box was a clear container with what looked like a coin collection. It looked like silver dollars. He quickly grabbed the container and placed that into the bag as well. Jake was now feeling a rush of adrenalin; it was thrilling.

Not wanting to be greedy, Jake decided he had enough booty to earn him at least a nice dinner with Stella. Thinking about Stella, he wondered where she was. Was she in the basement of this home too? As he walked into the hallway, he was immediately grabbed from behind.

"Thought you could steal my things eh?!!!" It was Mrs. Harrell who had grabbed him from behind. Jake started to struggle but he couldn't shake free.

"I THINK THE POLICE WILL WANT TO KNOW ABOUT THIS!!!" she yelled. Again Jake tried to get free. As he did so he could see the silhouette of someone at the end of the hall. Was it Stella? Whoever it was he couldn't worry about that now.

"You're not going anywhere my friend!" Jake continued to struggle. He could feel Mrs. Harrell trying to grab onto his ski mask, most likely in an effort to identify her burglar. Before she could, Jake kick her hard in the sin and then down on her foot and was able to shake loose. He dropped his bag and then ran as fast as he could to the den where he had left the window open for a quick escape. As he entered the den, he continued to run toward the widow that had been pried open. With his heart pounding, knowing that Mrs. Harrell was in hot pursuit, he straddled the window frame and then plunged to the ground below. As he hit the ground with a thud, he rolled for several feet. He regained his balance and quickly ran into the woods.

"I'll get you, you little bastard!!!" Jake could hear the far-off voice of Mrs. Harrell ringing in his head. He had quickly learned that Mrs. Harrell was no one to be trifled with.

Jake continued to run as fast as he could. He decided to run in an easterly direction to give the appearance that he wasn't staying in the neighborhood. As he got deep enough into the woods as not to be seen, he then headed back toward his house. When he reached the marsh toward the back of his property, he slowed down and took a deep breath. He looked back toward where Mrs. Harrell lived and looked to see if she was in pursuit. He could see some movement in the forest near her home and quickly hid behind a little burrow of marsh grass and a tree stump. He looked to see a dark figure appear. He started to tremble as he recognized it to be that of Mrs. Harrell. He had learned first-hand that Mrs. Harrell was quite strong. She was also a tall woman, and an intimidating figure.

As she neared, he lowered himself further and began to push himself into the marsh grass. He could feel water seeping into his jacket as he squashed himself further and further into to the marsh. He could hear Mrs. Harrell trampling the marsh grass as if she knew exactly where he was. She was no more than ten feet away when she came to an abrupt halt.

"Where is that bastard?" Mrs. Harrell muttered to herself. Jake tried to calm himself and slow his breathing, but he was too frightened. She stood there for what seemed like an hour to Jake but was really only ten minutes. She then turned and started walking back to her house. Jake waited until she was well into the forest and then slowly exhumed himself from the marshland. He walked back to his house, breathing a sigh of relief that he hadn't been caught. He took off the ski mask so he could breathe a little easier. He started to panic when he realized he had dropped the bag. Was there anything on or in the bag that might give away who the owner of it was? He felt confident that there was nothing that would identify him as the thief. He went into the house via the storm door and looked into Stella's room, half-hoping that she had returned. As he headed upstairs, he began to think about who the person was at the end of the hall in Mrs. Harrell's house. He didn't have a good look but could it have been Stella? It must have been since she went into the house the day before. What was she up to? The on-going mystery was becoming even more of a mystery.

******

The next day, after school, the KHP gathered in Mikaela's attic.

"Okay girls…and Zachary, I'm calling to order the 3rd meeting of the KHP. Now remember on Saturday we are doing a carwash for Sarah's Home for battered and abused women and children. I need all of you there so we can get a lot of cars washed. Will everyone be there?"

All the girls and Zachary silently nodded.

"Okay, I want everyone at Phil's Car Wash at 8 a.m. sharp." The girls, including Brittany, knew that Mikaela was now the undisputed leader of the group. She not only had the mental and emotional strength to be a leader, but most importantly the spiritual strength. It was clear she was tapping into a higher power.

"Okay, the next order of business. We need to heal the families in this town. We have too many divorces. Brittany, and now Mattie, I really feel for you guys. It's not easy coming from a broken home I know, but we can't just sit around and do nothing. We need to help others who have families that are being torn apart."

"Yeah, but how do we do that? We're not marriage counselors."

"Yeah, but there are other people we know. There's Mr. Philpot, the counselor at school."

"Isn't he just a guidance counselor?"

"No, he also does emotional counseling for kids that are having problems."

"How do you know that?"

"He counseled me."

"Don't you get counseled from…?" Brittany started to move her head and eyes in a bobbing motion pointing upward.

"Yes, but that doesn't mean that's the only way I get counsel. The Great Light uses others to help people see the light. Anyway, I want us to start fanning out during school. We are going to be counselors. We are going to help other kids going through the same issues."

"Yeah, but don't you need to be trained on counseling? I mean, I don't want someone committing suicide because of something I've said."

"That won't happen. People commit suicide because of what people haven't said. They commit suicide because they don't think anyone cares about them."

Brittany didn't seem so convinced. She kept hearing how different therapies were bad for different people; LGBTQ, people with severe depression, kids with bi-polar. All these groups needed specifically trained counselors to deal with their specific problems, not a bunch of kids.

"Look Brittany, I know what you're thinking and maybe you are right. But we cannot do nothing, we need to help other kids. That's what this group is about right?"

Brittany and the other girls began to nod their heads.

"Okay, so let's start identifying kids who come from divorced homes or that we know their parents are about to get a divorce."

"How do we do that?"

"We talk to them."

"Talk to a hundred kids?"

"Well twelve hundred if you include all the grades."

"How are we going to do that? We only see about hundred kids during lunch."

"You know we talk to other kids on the playground or walking to and from school. It doesn't just have to be the kids in our grade."

Brittany again conveyed a look of concern.

"Look, you're right. It will probably just be easier to talk with the kids in our grade. But don't limit yourself. Anyone you come in contact with; kids in our grade, kids in sixth grade, your family members, your aunts and uncles, someone on the street, all of these people may need your help sometime. All these people may be living in darkness, or shadow and they need to see the light."

Brittany began to think about her cousin Steve who committed suicide when she was young. Maybe had she been there for him he might have taken a different path. She was probably too young to make difference in his life, but now that she was older, she needed to help others. Every other girl had similar thoughts; people in their lives who were suffering and now it was time to step up and make a difference.

"Okay, here is tomorrow's assignment. You need to talk to one new person tomorrow and get to know them. Find out about how they are doing and just listen to them. Got it?"

"Got it!" came the unison response. The girls played in the attic with Zachary for a couple of hours before Mikaela excused herself to make dinner for her family.

******

Across town, Charlie was dealing with a different problem.

"Hey Jessie, how'ya doin'?"

Jessie looked at Charlie and walked by him without a response. She sat at her computer and started going through some online files. Charlie walked slowly over to her.

"Hey, can we talk?"

Jessie looked at Charlie and nodded.

"Can we go to the conference room?"

She again nodded and started walking toward the conference room with Charlie in tow. As they entered, Charlie closed the door behind him.

"Hey, I am really sorry for what happened the other night."

"I'm not sorry. I had fun."

"You looked a little sorry."

"I was unhappy because I knew you had regrets, but I didn't."

Charlie studied Jessie and wondered what she saw in him. She was a beautiful young woman who had her whole future ahead of her. Why would she risk it with an older man?

"Look, I really like you but…"

"But?"

"…but I love my wife and family and I cannot screw that up. It was wrong of me to do it. It was wrong of me to feel sorry for myself and to think that I could have a relationship with you."

"So it wasn't just sex?"

"Well it was about sex, but it was also about having a relationship. Look, I was really screwed up. I had thoughts that my wife was dying and feeling sorry for myself and so maybe I was thinking that I didn't want to be alone…not just that night but forever. I wanted someone like you in my life."

"In case your wife died?"

"Boy, as we talk about it I realize how disgusting that sounds. I realize how stupid I've been."

"You're not stupid. We're attracted to each other. Regardless of what's happening to your wife, it is important to be with the person you love right?" Jessie started to look deep into Charlie's eyes. He could not hold her gaze.

"So you were looking for more than just sex?" Charlie asked.

"Yes, I mean, there was a reason I got into bed with you. I really like you. Your warm, funny, we have a lot in common professionally."

"Yes, but don't you want someone your own age?"

"Youth is overrated as far as I'm concerned. I just want a caring, intelligent man in my life, he doesn't have to be my age."

Charlie looked at Jessie and admired her for her beliefs. But then he thought about Jayne. Regardless of Jessie's beliefs he knew it had been wrong to think his wife might lose her battle. It was wrong to not support her one hundred percent. He had let her down and he knew he had to correct the situation right then and there.

"Well, anyway, going forward, I think it best that we work separately."

"What do you mean?"

"I mean I assigned you to Cindy's team."

"Cindy? Cindy Pulaski?"

"Yeah, she has an opening on her project with Kahn Industries. They are building a new corporate center in Midtown and I recommended you for that."

Jessie was silent. She turned and looked away, breathing a long stream of air from her mouth. She then nodded, got up and walked away. From the conference room door Charlie could see Jessie going to her desk, picking up her bag and starting to walk out of the office. She stopped and looked at Charlie.

"Well, it was good working for you. I guess I'll report to Cindy in the morning?"

Charlie sighed and nodded. She took a long look at Charlie and shook her head. She then turned and walked away. Charlie leaned against the door frame and looked skyward. He knew he had done the right thing but still couldn't help but think about what might have been. Regardless of what might have been, he knew he had to take care of his wife and family; there was nothing more important.

******

At the basecamp of the Black Knights, Mac, Will and Jake met up. Jake was depressed about what was happening with Stella and sought counsel from the Knights.

"So where you been Jakey? Hangin' with your lady?" Mac said as he rubbed his jaw, remembering his encounter with Stella.

"I need to confess something to you guys and you are going to think it really weird."

Being the least forthcoming of the trio, Jake tended to be a listener versus storyteller so when Mac and Will heard that Jake wanted to make a confession, they were all ears. Jake hesitated, not sure if he really wanted to divulge his story to his friends.

"Go on Jake, what is it?" Will encourage Jake to speak.

"Well, you know Stella…it's not like we're really girlfriend and boyfriend."

"What are you then?"

"It's hard to explain."

"Oh God, she's not your sister is she?"

"No, no, no! Nothing like that! It's really weird though. We moved in last year to our house on Arendelle Court. We started cleaning up the place and when we did…I found her in the basement."

"You what?!!!" exclaimed Mac.

"I found her living in our basement."

"And your parents didn't know?"

"No. She wanted me to keep it a secret. She said she was hiding out away from her parents. She said they were abusing her so she ran-away. When she saw the house was for sale she broke in and started living in the basement."

"Wow, that's incredible!"

"Yeah, it is. So I've been keeping this secret from my parents and was just going along with it because…well, because I was getting to be with a girl, but now she's demanding things and not even staying at the house very often, it's weird."

"What kind of things is she demanding?"

"She wants me to steal things for her and take her out on fancy dates, it's weird right?"

"I don't know Jakey, she's pretty hot, I think I might do anything for her."

"Yeah, but steal?" Will asked Mac with a pained expression, remembering their adventure at the Harris house. Mac nodded knowing what Will was referring to.

"I don't know what to do. Do I tell the police, do I go to my parents?"

"No, don't do that. Just enjoy your time with her. She's a year older right? She'll probably leave soon; go to college, get a job."

"Well, she wants me to get a job right after high school so we can get an apartment together."

"Ya gotta go to college Jake," Will pleaded.

"Then the other day I saw her walking with the football team's quarterback and they looked pretty chummy."

"There you go. Just enjoy the time you have with her. She'll probably leave you for some hunky athlete or some fancy college guy. Just enjoy the sex and don't worry about it," Mac said, handing Jake a joint. For the rest of the meeting, Jake remained silent, pondering his next move, while Mac and Will talked about the latest video game that had come out.

******

The next day at school, Mikaela met the girls for lunch at the cafeteria. She told them to fan out and meet some new people. The KHP did as requested and the girls introduced themselves to other 5th grade groups. They got on especially well with the boys at their soccer club and drew some converts to their cause that day. They quickly learned that many families were in trouble. Many of the kid's parents were in various stages of divorce, or counseling or fighting and it was clear that many of the children there were feeling hurt and insecure. The girls encouraged many of the kids to seek counseling and to not keep things bottled up. Mikaela had created little index cards that had the counselor's names as well as various other off-campus counselors with their contact information.

As Mikaela walked around the cafeteria looking for kids to talk to, she noticed Billy O'Connell sitting by himself which was unusual. Mikaela had had a crush on Billy for a long time. They were close friends growing up. Prior to moving to Arendelle Court, the Royaltons had lived in a different neighborhood close to Billy's house. Mikaela and Billy played soccer together in the neighborhood and were at the same soccer club. Both were the best players at the club, being selected to play on the National Regional team.

"Hey Mickey, how ya doing?"

"Good Billy, haven't talked to you in a long time."

"Yeah, well, they got me travelin' everywhere for soccer. We just got back from New York last weekend."

"Wow, really, that must have been fun?"

"No, not really. It was an eight-hour drive with a bunch of other smelly soccer players."

Mikaela burst out laughing. She never was afraid of boys but with Billy she always felt a little nervous. He wasn't like other boys. Despite being a great soccer player, he was humble and loving and always willing to help anyone. That's why she loved him.

"How are things going at home? How's your mom and dad?"

"Ok, I guess. I don't see my mom much these days. She's always flying somewhere for business. My dad works a lot. My brother and sister are both away at college so it gets pretty quiet around. How are you doing? I heard you quit the club."

"I'm doing really good. I didn't have much time for soccer with homework and the KHP."

"KHP, what's that?'

"It's a little club me and the girls formed. It's just about us kids helping people. We're going around today to introduce ourselves and see if anyone has any problems."

"That sounds pretty cool. Is it a church thing?"

"No, just thought we'd help out anyone who needs help. Do you want to join?"

"Who else is in the club?"

"Well, right now it's just me, my little brother, Brittany, Mattie, Marnie, Lola, Becky and Greta."

"Who's Greta?"

"She's a girl in the 4th grade."

"Cool. Sound fun. What do we do?"

"Want to help us with a carwash on Saturday?"

"Love to but I got a soccer game. In fact, with soccer and homework I don't think I will have time."

Mikaela studied Billy closely. She could tell he was feeling lonely.

"Look Billy, school and soccer are not everything. You need to get out and be with people. You're stuck at home I can tell. Come with us."

Billy was quiet. What Mikaela was saying was the truth. He had poured so much time into soccer and now he was feeling burned out with the constant practicing, games and traveling. He wanted something different.

"Well, let me think about it."

Mikaela smiled and put her hand on his shoulder. She gave him a wink and then walked away. Billy turned and looked at Mikaela. Mikaela was a special girl and he thought it might be a good idea to help her. Life at home was routine and he was needing something more. Maybe helping the KHP was the answer.

CHAPTER 15

Darkness Sets In

As fall approached, Mikaela became concerned that she wouldn't be able to visit heaven soon. Things were going well at school and the KHP were starting to have impact not only in school but in the community. News was not all good however as Jayne was starting to become ill again and was having another recurrence of the cancer. She had to go back to the clinic for chemo as that seemed to be the only treatment now working. Mikaela and Zachary tried to bury their concern by focusing on the KHP and school. In Jake's case, he spent more time smoking pot and thinking of ways he could win over Stella. For Charlie, he was stepping up and helping more at home. Between he and his mother-in-law, they were able to keep a good eye on Jayne.

The mood at school was starting to change. Many kids were now going to the school counselor on a regular basis. While it was good for the kids, it caught the attention of Principal Wilson. She soon learned who was the cause of the new uptick in children coming to the school counselor and she was none too pleased.

On the first Saturday of September, the KHP met at Sarah's House, bringing the supplies they had earned via the carwash earlier the month before. As Mikaela walked in with her large bag of canned goods, she stopped in her tracks, looking at a girl coming down the stairway. Zachary placed his hand on her arm and they both looked at each other.

"Hi, do you remember me?"

Both Mikaela and Zachary nodded their heads.

"My name is Karyn. Karyn Soleski. I was the girl you talked to in front of the abortion clinic several months ago. I want to thank you for talking to me. After I went into the clinic, the strangest thing happened to me. It was as if someone was talking to me. A voice was telling me to get out of there as fast as I could. It was telling me I needed to have my baby. That I had life inside of me and I needed to protect it."

Mikaela and Zachary were dumbfounded. They thought for sure that she had gone in determined to have her abortion. Large grins began to simultaneously form on Mikaela's and

Zachary's faces. Karyn set her baby down in a nearby crib and walked back over to Mikaela and Zachary and gave them a great big hug.

"Wow, Karyn, we are so happy you chose life. There's nothing more important."

"I know and you taught me that."

"What will you be doing?"

"Well, Mr. Snyder, you know 'Walt' from across the street at the homeless shelter is going to give me computer lessons a couple of days a week so I can learn programming. I want to become a computer programmer; make games and stuff."

"Wow, that's awesome Karyn. I think you are heading in the right direction."

"And all because of you."

"Glad we could help."

As Mikaela said this she was stunned to see another person coming down the stairs. It was Billy O'Connell brining down some furniture.

"Hey Billy, what are you doing here? I thought were playing soccer on Saturdays?"

"Yeah, but I quit. I learned there are other things in life besides soccer."

"What did your parents say?"

"Well, my dad was not too happy. He said 'how'ya gonna pay for college?' I just told him that I'll get good grades and get a scholarship that way. Anyway, I want to be doctor, not a soccer player."

"That's great Billy and thanks for helping us."

"No problem."

The children had a great day at the women's shelter and felt they were really helping the community and single unwed mothers. As it turns out they were really helping everywhere, especially at school. But the following Monday Principal Wilson called in Mikaela to talk about her "helping" the school.

"Miss Royalton. Looks like we meet again?'

"Yes, Principal Wilson, how can I help you?"

"Well you can help me by stop helping."

"I'm sorry, what do you mean?"

"This little club of yours…the KHP?"

"What about it?"

"You have to shut it down."

"Why?"

"This club is causing a disruption to families. I have a whole bunch of parents calling me telling me their kids were told to stop doing sports or other activities so they could join your club to help others. They think it's a cult or something."

"We're just trying to help people. Help families who are struggling with divorce and broken homes."

"That is not your job Mikaela. It is the job of professional counselors."

"Yes and that is what we are doing. We are identifying troubled kids and suggesting that they go to the school counselor or other professional counselors so they don't bottle things up."

"It is not your job to decide who needs to go to counseling or not. Individuals have to decide that on their own."

"Kids don't know they need help. They just think their parents arguing is a normal thing."

"Look Mikaela, I'm going to tell you once. You have really ticked me off. It's not your job to tell anyone they need counseling. Just because you think someone is in trouble doesn't mean they need counseling. There are all kinds of families here; families with one mother or one father, maybe two mothers and two fathers and because you do not feel a family fits into that category doesn't mean you have the right to tell them to go get help."

Mikaela was stunned and near tears. She took solace in the fact that she knew what she was doing was right, but the fact that an older adult was accusing her of being in the wrong was hard to take.

"Now, I want you to shut down this club right now or you are going to be suspended."

Mikaela stood up and walked out of the room. She felt numb as she maneuvered out of the office not acknowledging anyone as she walked back to her classroom. What was she going to do? She couldn't disband the club. It wasn't right.

Back at the house, Jake spotted his dad in the kitchen.

"Hey dad, how you doing?"

"Okay. Making some dinner for your mom."

"Looks, ah, very healthy."

"Yeah, not very appetizing I'm afraid. I'll order us some pizza in a minute."

"Hey dad, can I talk to you for a minute."

"Sure son, what it is?"

Jake gathered his courage. He hadn't spoken to his dad about girls or dating before.

"Could I borrow some money for this Friday night?"

"What's it for?"

"Well, I'm taking this girl out for dinner."

"Oh yeah, that's why you needed the SUV? I thought you were taking her out several weeks ago? What happened?"

"Oh, we couldn't coordinate our schedules."

"How much do you need?"

"A hundred."

"A hundred. Where are you taking this girl?"

"That nice Italian restaurant on Main Street."

"Tell ya what, I'll give you sixty and then a month's advance on your allowance."

"It's a deal!"

Jake grabbed his dad's hand to shake. Charlie, not used to much emotion from Jake was taken aback. As he shook Jake's hand, he realized that he had not worked hard enough to understand what his son had been going through. He remembered not being too close to his father. His father wanting him "to be a man," whatever that meant. Did being a man mean to not cry, to be able to physically fight a bully? What did "being a man" really mean? He realized in that moment he had not taught Jake much of anything. Apart from helping him with his homework and driving him to soccer games, he realized he had fallen short as a father. At that moment, the light hit him and he endeavored to do better. He pulled Jake into him to give him a hug. Jake himself was surprised. He was not used to any physical displays of love from his father. As Charlie clutched his son, he promised himself he would do better.

"So, tell me about this girl."

Jake thought for a moment, not wanting to divulge that "this girl" had been a tenant in the basement for almost a year.

"She's great. I think you'll like her."

Charlie smiled. He was glad his son looked happy. He realized that he should have been encouraging Jake to do more social activities like school dances or dates. Jake smiled at his dad, nodded and then headed back upstairs. He felt like now he had a chance to win back Stella. Later that night, Jake snuck down to the basement to see if Stella had returned. She was not there. He decided to send her a text. The tablet he gave her, or stole for her, had texting capabilities, so he decided to contact her…

Where are you?

He waited the rest of the night but there was no reply. The next morning he did receive a text.

I'm at a friend's house. What's going on?

Jake was surprised that Stella could be so casual. It seemed like the year he had helped her while in the basement meant nothing.

I wanted to ask you out on that date for Friday. Do you still want to go?

Yeah, that would be awesome! Where are we going?

There's an Italian restaurant on Main Street called Ristorante di Vittorio

Sounds great. What time?

8pm. Do you want me to pick you up?

No that's okay. I'll meet you there

Although finding Stella a little aloof, Jake was happy he had a chance to meet with her and hopefully impress her.

******

After school, Mikaela and Zachary were walking home. They noticed a boy sitting on a park bench, almost in the exact same position Becky was several months earlier. Mikaela recognized him as a boy in the sixth grade. He had been crying.

"Are you okay?"

The boy looked over at Mikaela and nodded.

"What's the matter?" she asked in her usual direct manner.

"Ah, well, I was just thinking about my dad."

"What's wrong with him?'

"He died a couple of years ago. On this day…two years ago. I really miss him."

Mikaela sat down on the bench next to him. He looked over at her and could see she was totally focused on him and his pain. Zachary was still learning about patience when his sister would sit and interact with people. He still had the urge to run off and play, but he was slowly learning.

"Tell me about him."

The boy began to think long and hard, remembering everything about his dad.

"He was great; kind, loving, funny. He was a great prankster. I remember this one time, when he had this friend of his who was a police officer show up at our house one night. My older brother had gotten a traffic ticket but didn't seem to really care. The police officer gave my brother such a chewing out and was getting his handcuffs out to arrest him – my brother was freaking out! Then my dad comes in and starts bursting out in laughter. Boy…my brother never had another ticket after that."

As the boy remembered his father, tears began to well up in his eyes. Mikaela put her hand on his shoulder to try and comfort him. The boy looked over at her and could see she meant well.

"You're Mikaela right? The girl in that club?"

Mikaela nodded her head. She began to think if "that club" was going to be around much longer and it pained her.

"You're Phillip Sommerville right?"

The boy nodded. Mikaela had a great memory. She often poured over the year books from school to get familiar with various students. She recognized him from a school play he had been in.

"Look Phillip, just know that your dad is loved and living in the light."

"Is that heaven?"

She nodded her head.

"And, it's a wonderful place; no pain, no stress, only love."

"Wow, sounds great. I'd like to go there now and find my dad. I really miss him. He used to talk to me all the time and help me with my problems."

"Just know that he still loves you and he is actually still helping you. Just because you are separated doesn't mean he is not alive. He is alive and he loves you very much."

At that point the sun seemed to shine more brightly. Phillip did feel loved and had a warm feeling, a feeling like his father was watching over him. He smiled at Mikaela and nodded. He picked up his backpack and started to walk home. Before he left, he turned back to speak to Mikaela.

"Hey, thank you. I appreciate it."

Mikaela nodded and smiled.

After Phillip left, Mikaela and Zachary decided to take a shortcut home through Becky's yard. As they turned the corner to their cul-de-sac, they saw an ambulance in their driveway. They began to run home. Their mother was on a stretcher and being placed into the ambulance.

"Dad, what's happening?"

"Your mother had a tumble down the stairs. She was unconscious for a while. C'mon, let's get in the car and drive over to the hospital."

The ambulance pulled out of the driveway and headed for the hospital with Charlie and the children in hot pursuit. When they arrived they took her into the ER leaving Charlie and the children waiting anxiously outside. After finishing the usual paperwork with the clerk, Charlie called Jake to let him know what was going on. Jake got into his car and arrived shortly after. Everyone waited for a couple of hours before a doctor finally came out to meet with them.

"Sorry it took so long. Your wife and mother is in stable condition but we need to run some more tests. Can you tell me what happened?"

"Ah, yes, I had helped her to the bathroom. She said she wanted to go down to the kitchen to move around a bit. I asked her if it was a good idea and she said she would like to. I told her to wait while I went down to the kitchen to take some plates to put in the sink. I heard her at the top of the stairs asking for some help. I went over but before I got there she had already tumbled down most of the stairs. She was unconscious and I tried to revive her. I carried her to the sofa in my den and then called 911."

"Sounds like she over did it and passed out."

"Yeah, I could kick myself. I should have waited by the bathroom and helped her down.'

"Don't do that dad," Mikaela said as she placed her hand on his arm. "You didn't know she was going to try and come down the stairs by herself."

"I think your daughter's right. She probably felt strong enough to go to the top of the stairs but then lost her balance, passed out."

Charlie looked at his daughter and took comfort. She seemed to be years beyond her age and was the rock of the family. He smiled at his daughter and gave her hug. Mikaela knew that her father had corrected his path and was now fully engaged in the family. Now if they could only get their mother well, life would be perfect.

For the next two days the family slept in Jayne's hospital room. The family kept vigil as they waited for her to wake up. Later in the afternoon of the second day, she regained consciousness. Her eyes began to blink and a small smile appeared on her face. Her eyes slowly opened. She was happy to see her family. While the family was grateful she had regained consciousness, they were saddened to learn that Jayne's cancer had spread. Her outlook was becoming bleaker. The family stayed with her the rest of the afternoon and then left for home after visiting hours. The family drove home without a single word being spoken in the car.

******

Despite everything that was going on with his mother, Jake took solace that on Friday he would have a chance to make things right with Stella. He walked home from school that afternoon with butterflies in his stomach, planning everything in his head for the next evening.

Back at the house, Mikaela and Zachary sat nervously on the floor of the attic playing with toys. Mikaela looked at the sun and waited for it to appear in the ceiling window. When it did, she and Zachary stood back and watched the beams of light hit the back of the room. The portal appeared and they hurriedly ran to open it. They immediately flung it open and ran into the field. There was a feeling of fresh air that they hadn't felt in a long time. They immediately floated up into the air and were soon flying along. They were back in heaven.

In previous trips to paradise, there had not been any real plan to it, they were just there to learn and have fun. Now though they were there on a mission – to heal their mother.

As they arrived at the Temple of Light, they were greeted by the orbs who were happy to see them. They were also introduced to a new orb – Greta.

"Greta, wow, you're an angel now?"

"Not really an angel more like a 'child of light'"

"So you are no longer on Earth?"

"Yes, my mission is done there."

"What was your mission?"

"To lead you to the light."

Mikaela was so happy. She now realized that her friend Greta was really a supernatural being who had come to help her during difficult times. The two embraced and Mikaela felt such a warm feeling, similar to what she felt near Mother Light.

"Where is Mother Light? I need to talk with her."

"She is over by the Great Chrystal Orb. She knew you were coming for a particular reason. You can go to her."

"Where do we go?"

"Just head for the Great Light and you will see her."

Mikaela smiled at Greta and gave her another hug, or what was the equivalent of a hug in heaven. It was more of an exchange of spiritual energy. At that point Mikaela and Zachary began winging their way toward the Great Light. They had never gone beyond the Temple of Light before. If it were somehow possible, heaven was even more beautiful beyond the Temple of Light. There was even more love and more understanding as they flew toward the Great Light. For what seemed a million miles, they finally arrived at a beautiful crystal lake with a shimmering waterfall. Along the banks of the lake was Mother Light standing next to a giant oak tree.

"Mother Light, we have been looking for you."

"Yes, I know children and I know why you have come. You want to heal your mother."

"Yes, Mother Light, how do we do that?"

Mother Light began to point to a small beam of light that was just under one of the branches of the oak tree. As she pointed to it the beam of light turned into an orb. The orb grew and grew until it filled the length and height of their minds and souls – they could not see anything other than Mother Light and the great orb. Mother Light then seemed to pull something out of the orb. It was a small gold box. It looked like a box that a man would give to a woman as an engagement ring. Mother Light then turned and handed it to Mikaela.

"My child. This is a small box, but inside it is something special, something that will help your family. You can only open it twice. You will need to use it twice for your family to save them. Do you understand?"

"Yes, Mother Light."

"When you need to use it you simply open the box. That is all you do."

"Yes Mother, we understand."

"Good. Now go my children. Your family needs you."

The children hugged Mother Light and were soon off again flying back home. Mikaela clutched onto the gold box firmly and when she arrived back in the attic quickly placed it underneath the pillow in her bed for safekeeping. Zachary wanted to look inside but Mikaela reminded him that they could only open the box twice. Zachary was saddened he couldn't convince his sister otherwise.

******

The next evening, Jake prepared for his date with Stella. He was nervous and ended up taking two showers. He had bought some cheap cologne and splashed it all over his body. It was musk and he had heard it attracted women. He was unsure of the veracity of the claim but was willing to try anything at that point. He dug through his closet looking for a suit his parents had bought him that he had used for his grandfather's funeral a couple of years earlier and hoped it still fit. It was large back then so hopefully he hadn't grown too much since.

As he struggled to get on his suit, he looked at himself in the mirror. He had a few new pimples and they were making him feel a lack of confidence. Stella was beautiful. How did he think the deserved to be with her? As he looked in the mirror he could feel himself trembling. He worked diligently at tying his tie and eventually gave up and decided to google *how to tie a tie*. He decided to forgo the tie and hoped the vest that came with the suit would give him a satisfactory appearance of sophistication.

At the bottom of Jake's closet he located some old black shoes. He grabbed a t-shirt that was also on the floor and began to polish the shoes. He breathed on the shoes and began to apply pressure hoping that somehow they would become shiny. He had to settle for a dull blackish-gray. He continued to study his facial expression in the mirror and decided he better get high for his date. He went over to his dresser and opened the top drawer. In the top drawer was his wallet and inside of that was a squashed joint. He had matches inside a model army tank that was on top of the drawer. He went to his bedroom window and opened hit. He lit a match and then set flame to the end of his joint. He sat on the edge of his bed and blew a long stream of smoke from his mouth out of the window. His grandmother was downstairs watching his siblings and he hoped the smell would not drift below.

After five minutes of smoking his joint, he heard his grandmother at his bedroom door.

"Jake, I smell a bunch of smoke. Is everything okay?"

Panicked, Jake ran over to the window and threw the joint out. He ran over to his closet and grabbed a towel and began to swing it around wildly to try and get rid of the smoke.

"Jake, is everything alright?" came the muffled voice of Nanna Jean.

"Yeah, grandma. I think Mr. Hill is burning some leaves next door and the wind is blowing this way."

As he said that, the fire alarm in the house started to ring out. The nice buzz he was feeling was now completely obliterated from his being and he had to increase the reps of the towel. He moved the curtains away from his window and as he did so he could see a small fire smoldering in the backyard. He realized he had thrown the joint into a pile of dead leaves. He immediately ran downstairs, passed his grandmother and siblings and ran out into the backyard. He grabbed the garden hose and began to spray water all over the pile of leaves until a small tributary was created. Finally convinced that the fire was extinguished, he turned off the hose and headed back into the house. Waiting at the doorway was his grandmother and brother and sister.

"What in the world happened Jake?"

"Oh nothing. It's pretty dry out. I think Mr. Hill was burning some leaves and maybe a cinder came over the fence and landed in the leaves there."

Assuring himself he had made up a good lie, he walked back into the house. As he passed Mikaela, he could see he had not convinced her and that she probably knew what had really happened.

"Well, you better hurry up for your date," his grandmother exhorted him.

"Yeah, yeah. Just leaving."

Jake grabbed the car keys that were in a bowl by the front door and waved a weak hand toward the family that had assembled to see him off.

"Bye Jake. Be good," said Mikaela.

Jake nodded his head with a very glum look on his face.

"Boy, is he going on a date or going to a funeral," a surprisingly apt observation came from Zachary.

As Jake drove down the street toward downtown, he searched the glove compartment and console for any pot he might have stashed away. Since his dad had taken the SUV he had to resort to taking his own car which turned out to be better given the car's hidden valuables. He eventually found the small remains of an extinguished joint and pulled over to the parking lot of an abandoned warehouse where he quickly lit up. As he sat in the car wondering if the date was worth all the stress, he saw a police car driving by rather slowly on Main Street. He almost jumped out of his skin when he saw the patrol car go by. He then slumped over to the passenger side of his car and as he did so threw the joint out of the window. He turned on the ignition and sped away to the other side of the parking lot that exited on

Pioneer Parkway. He hoped his abrupt departure hadn't alerted the cop.

Jake decided to forgo any further attempt at intoxicating himself and headed to the restaurant. He pulled into the parking lot and parked at the furthest end he could find in an effort to check his appearance and demeanor before entering the restaurant. He could feel his heart pounding in his chest as he took one last look at himself in the mirror. He took comfort in the past that Stella had found him attractive enough to kiss him, but maybe she had grown tired of his looks and his juvenile attempts at romance. The alternating self-doubt and self-exhortation was making his head spin. Was he about to pass out?

Jake entered the restaurant and was greeted by a hostess.

"Good evening…Jake? Jake is that you?"

It was Belinda Simmons from high school. Belinda was a senior but she had played soccer in the past and knew Jake from the club.

"Haven't seen you in a while."

"No, it has been a while. How are you?" a completely disinterested and highly distracted Jake asked.

"Great. I'm heading to Stanford next year on a soccer scholarship. I'm just trying to earn a little spending money before I go. Can't wait to finally get out of this Podunk town."

"Yeah, yeah, that sounds great," Jake said, not listening and having his head on a swivel looking around for Stella.

"Did you have a reservation Jake?"

"Ah, yeah…"

The hostess waited for further elaboration. Jake noticed that she was looking rather intently at him.

"…ah, for 8 o'clock under Royalton."

"Oh yeah, Jake Royalton. I couldn't remember your last name. Are you still playing soccer?"

Jake continued to look around outside to see if Stella would show up.

"Oh, ah, yeah. I play a little. I think I might be quitting…"

Just then Stella walked in. She was wearing a short black dress with matching high heels and a shawl. She looked incredible. Jake's eyes began to enlarge and his tongue practically fell out of his mouth.

"Wow, you look great!" Jake practically yelled. He looked around to see if he had caused any commotion with his observations.

"Why thank you Jakey. Do we have a table?"

"Yes you do, right this way please," the hostess said grabbing a couple of menus. As they reached a nice table in the center of the restaurant, a waiter met the couple and pulled the chair out for Stella. Stella was duly impressed.

"Good evening sir and madame. Tonight's special is a spicy linguini and clams. Would you like to start off with any appetizers; calamari, mozzarella sticks?"

Jake looked at Stella with a smile and raised his eyebrows in an effort to nonverbally ask if she wanted appetizers.

"Sure, mozzarella sticks sound great."

"Excellent. Now I assume you are both underage?"

Both nodded their heads in unison.

"Would you like anything to drink of a non-alcoholic nature? We have a nice chilled sparkling apple cider, soda, etc."

"Just water for me," Jake said.

"I'll try the apple cider," Stella said giving her order with a bright smile.

"Excellent, madame. I'll get your drinks and be right back."

As the two studied their menus, Jake would periodically look up at Stella. She looked incredible. She was the most beautiful girl he had ever seen. She sensed that he was looking at her and she would look up and catch him just looking away. She would smile a little knowing smile. Jake stared at the menu but nothing seemed to register with him. He was too nervous to think about food.

Eventually the waiter returned with their drinks and a basket of bread.

"Have you two decided?"

"Yes, I'll have the chicken alfredo," Stella said, raising her eyebrows at Jake and offering him a flirtatious smile.

"And for you sir?"

"Ah, I'll have…" Jake had not really looked at the menu and just picked the quickest thing he could find.

"…the spinach florentine."

"Hmmm, interesting choice," the waiter said. Stella also looking a little surprised at his choice. As the waiter walked away, Jake began to look intently at Stella.

"So, how have you been?"

"Great, and you?"

"Hanging in there. My mom is back in the hospital."

"Oh, that's too bad. You poor thing."

"I've really missed you."

"You have?" Stella said with a knitted brow. "I haven't been gone more than a few days."

"Yeah, but it feels like a lifetime. Do you not like it at the house anymore?"

"No, I do. It's just I have a friend that likes me to stay with her."

"What friend?" Jake asked with a suspicious tone, thinking the "friend" was really the jock from high school.

"Ah, she's someone from my old school. You wouldn't know her."

"Oh, okay," Jake said, pretending to be understanding.

"Anyway, how's school going?"

"Better, I'm getting my grades up and hopefully with a good score on the SAT I'll be able to go to the university."

"Great. Maybe you can get a job and we can get an apartment together."

"Yeah, I don't know if my parents would go for that."

"Maybe we could go out of state then?"

"Maybe. My mom's still technically employed by the university and so I can get most of my tuition covered."

Stella looked a little sad as she took a sip of her sparkling apple cider that the waiter had just delivered to the table. Jake tried to find a way to cheer her up.

"We'll see. Maybe we can get an apartment. It's just my parents have certain ideas about unmarried people living together."

"Why?"

"I don't know. I just remember that my mom would get angry with my aunt for living with this guy. Then she got really mad with her when she got pregnant. I just remember a lot of conversations and arguments where my mom said it wasn't right for her to be living with a man without a commitment, or being married."

"Wow, sounds antiquated."

"Yeah, I guess. But my aunt always seemed to go from one terrible relationship to another. She got pregnant twice…I think she had an abortion. She's got one kid and she never could go back to college. She's living in a bad part of town."

"Well, we won't let that happen to us," Stella said as she clutched Jake's hand and began to rub it.

CHAPTER 16

Mikaela's Race

Back at the house, Mikaela began having a feeling that something was happening to her mother. She sensed that the light and life were slowly leaving her. She had to get to the hospital. She ran downstairs and asked her grandmother to take her to the hospital.

"No dear, we cannot go to the hospital. Your father is there now and he will call us if there is anything the matter."

"But nanna, something is wrong with mom. I need to get to the hospital."

"No dear. I need to stay here with your brother. We will go first thing in the morning, right after breakfast."

Mikaela tried to control the hysteria that was slowly brewing inside of her. She then walked upstairs to her bedroom and retrieved the gold box from under her pillow. She put it in her backpack and grabbed her cellphone and slipped downstairs and into the garage undetected. She opened the garage door, got on her bike and peddled as fast as she could to the hospital.

Back at the restaurant, the waiter was serving Jake and Stella their food. Stella looked down at her plate with glee while Jake contemplated what he had ordered. It looked awfully green and he now wished he had been more intent when looking at the menu. His dismay soon passed however with one look at Stella. Even when she ate her food she looked incredibly sexy. She had a little more eyeliner on than usual. She also used a little bit more mascara and a peach color lip gloss. Her hair was tied back with a ribbon but parted on the side so some of the blonde strands almost covered her right eye. She was an angel.

As Mikaela arrived at the hospital, she dropped her bike on the lawn in front of the entrance and ran as fast as she could. She was greeted by one of the nurses at the entrance who knew her. Mikaela explained why she was there but the nurse wasn't convinced and just explained she could only see her mother for another thirty minutes before visitors had to leave. They had made an exception for her father to stay overnight but that was it.

Mikaela took the elevator up to the 7th floor of the hospital and as soon as the door opened she ran down the hall to her mother's room. Inside the room, she could see her mother hooked-up to a ventilator as well as a myriad of other wires and tubes. Her father was passed out on a cot on the other side of her mother's bed. He had been up the previous twenty-four hours and was sound asleep. As Mikaela neared her mother's bed, she placed her hand on her mother's hand. She began to sob uncontrollably because she knew that life was leaving her mother. Her mother looked peaceful, but she was getting cold to the touch. As Mikaela looked around the room she sensed a darkness, not just because it was night but there was something more. It was devoid of true light. There were machines that were pulsating with artificial light and a small bedside lamp was on, but there was a feeling of darkness. Mikaela then grabbed her backpack and opened it. She pulled out the gold box and placed it on her mother's bed. She went back and closed the door to the room and then back again to her mother's bed. She then picked up the box and began meditating on Mother Light's face. She then opened the box. As she opened the box, the most incredible light filled the room. It seemed even brighter than the light in heaven. Coming out of the box was pure energy and light and it felt like she had just unleashed a tidal wave of water surging throughout the room. The walls began to pulsate with light and the room started to violently shake. Mikaela thought the room was coming apart and contemplated closing the box. Something told her however to keep the box open. The longer she kept the box open the more pure energy and light would fill the room and fill her mother. As Mikaela looked at her mother, it was as if she could see the light being absorbed into her body. She could see inside of her body and that the light was healing her. Her mother's body began to shake and vibrate and Mikaela became frightened thinking that it was like someone being possessed by a demon. The longer she held the box open however, she began to feel the warmth and the love of the light. She herself became stronger by the light and she knew that what she was doing was healing her mother.

As Mikaela continued to hold the box open, a voice told her that it was sufficient and that she should close the box. As she closed the box the room immediately returned to its original state, with nothing disturbed. Mikaela waited patiently for her mother to respond. After a couple of minutes, her mother's eyes began to flicker and finally open. Her mother looked around the room and smiled. She then looked over to see Mikaela and then began to shake with tears of joy. She took off the ventilator mask and sat up in bed.

"Mikaela, what happened?"

"I healed you mom."

"You healed me? How?"

"It's something someone taught me how to use."

"What's going on?" a rather groggy Charlie asked as he slowly got up from the cot. He had been awoken by the commotion.

"I feel incredible honey."

"What? How?" a completely stunned Charlie asked.

"I don't know. Mikaela said she learned a technique or something to heal me."

Charlie looked at Mikaela and started to scratch his head. For quite some time he had learned not to underestimate his daughter, but now she had the power to heal? He could not quite wrap his mind around that one.

"What's going on in here?" one of the nurses asked.

"I'm recovered nurse. I feel better than I did before I got sick!" Jayne exclaimed. The puzzled nurse slipped back out of the room and walked briskly to find the doctor on duty. She waved down Dr. Soto and the doctor hurriedly joined the panicked nurse. The two entered the room and could not believe their eyes. The doctor, not having disclosed anything to the patient and family, had been convinced that Jayne was only days from succumbing to her illness. But now she was sitting up in bed and completely animated, talking with her husband and daughter.

"Wow, you look remarkable Mrs. Royalton," the doctor said in a perplexed tone.

"I feel fantastic doctor."

"How did this happen?"

"I don't know. My daughter says she was taught a technique of some kind."

Everyone looked intently at Mikaela. Mikaela looked into her backpack and could see the gold box lying at the bottom. The doctor stood there in disbelief. She had never seen anything so remarkable.

"I feel so great, I want to get out of bed and walk."

"I don't know if that is a good idea dear?" Charlie asked still completely stunned. The doctor and nurse were not so sure either but before they could even object, Jayne was pulling off the covers and getting out of bed. The nurse started pulling off the tubes and sensors connected to her. She stood up, stretched her arms and then starting walking around the room.

"I can't believe it. I haven't had this much exercise in over a year."

Back at the restaurant, Jake and Stella had finished their dinners. The waiter asked if they would like any dessert and they both declined with Jake anxiously asking for the check.

"Well Mr. Royalton, I think you've earned yourself a night of unbridled lovemaking," Stella said with a wink. Jake welled up with pride, knowing that he had accomplished what he had set out to do. He was feeling more confident than ever before, until the waiter brought him the check. It appeared he had enough to cover the dinner but he could tell he didn't have much over for the tip. With a sly smile, Stella pushed a twenty-dollar bill across the table to Jake. Jake sighed and smiled. It wasn't the way he wanted things to go but it was better than not tipping a somewhat snobbish waiter. The couple then exited the restaurant arm-in-arm, Jake saying goodnight to his old soccer buddy. The couple walked over to the car and Jake opened the passenger side door for Stella.

"So how did you get here tonight?"

"My friend who I had been staying with brought me."

Jake nodded and got into the car. They drove slowly through downtown on Main Street, Jake bursting with pride knowing he had with him the most beautiful girl in the world.

At the hospital, while Dr. Soto was examining Jayne, Mikaela was being interrogated by multiple nurses as to how she had healed her mother. She tried to explain that through prayer and positive thinking she had healed her. She felt it would be too difficult to understand that she had a magic gold box and that the light it emitted had healed her mom. As she continued to talk to the nurses she again had another premonition. This time it was about Jake. She knew that he was in trouble and needed her help.

"I'm sorry, but I need to go. My brother needs my help."

"Wait Mikaela, I'll drive you," her father yelled as Mikaela disappeared around the corner. As she ran down the hall and into the elevator, she pulled her cellphone from her backpack and called her grandmother."

"Nanna."

"Mikaela? Where are you?"

"I'm at the hospital."

"Young lady, didn't I…"

"Nanna, not now. Please put Zach on the phone."

"Listen, this is no way…"

"Nanna, please, we have no time."

Nanna Jean was angry and perplexed but she gave in to Mikaela's request and put Zachary on the phone.

"Hey Mikaela, what's up?"

"Zach. I think Jake is in trouble or about to be in trouble. He should be returning home from his date soon so keep an eye on him. He'll probably try and go down to the basement. See if you can find him."

Just as Mikaela and Zachary were talking, Jake and Stella parked down in the street near Mrs. Harrell's house. There was an alley way that was on the southside of Mrs. Harrell's house that led to a communications building and an electrical generator that were all fenced off. Jake parked the car near the fenced off area where no one could see it from the cul-de-sac. They feared they would be seen if they pulled up into the Royalton driveway. The couple then ran back down the alley and up the cul-de-sac to Jake's house, running around back and then sneaking into the storm door.

When Jake and Stella got inside, they ran over to the room and opened the door. What was inside completely surprised Jake. It was Mrs. Harrell and she had Zachary. Zachary had been bound and gagged.

"Hey what is this?"

Mrs. Harrell ran over to Jake and grabbed him from behind, placing her hand over his mouth. Jake tried to struggle but she was very strong. Stella grabbed a piece of cloth and wrapped it tightly over his mouth. While Mrs. Harrell held his arms behind him, Stella began to tie him up with rope.

"There that ought to take care of you," Stella said with a wicked look in her eyes. Jake squirmed and tried to loosen his bonds but to no avail.

"So, you thought you could come into my house and steal things did you?" Mrs. Harrell said with an evil scowl.

"You know what I do to boys who are bad? I make sure they are not bad ever again."

The boys continued to struggle while Mrs. Harrell and Stella began to move aside the metal framed shelving that had been in the room. Once moved to the side, it revealed something like a trapdoor. Stella pulled up the trapdoor and looked down. She then turned to the boys and began to laugh with an awful cackle.

"You see boys, Stella is my daughter. She's lived with me in the house down the street for years. I told everyone she had gone to boarding school, but in reality she was living down here. You see, this area all belonged to my family before we were swindled out of it. We owned the neighborhood and the mines. Down there is one of our coal processing plants. So we plotted and decided we would take back what was ours."

As Mrs. Harrell continued to speak, Stella tied a length of rope onto the rope that had be wrapped around Jake's torso. In this fashion she could now pull him. He tried to struggle and call for help but he had been tightly bound and gagged.

He knew his grandmother was just upstairs but it was to no avail. Stella began to pull him toward the trapdoor.

"It's so funny that you thought I could be your girlfriend. Foolish, foolish boy," Stella said with a fiendish delight. Her eyes seemed to be ablaze, like she was possessed. Stella slowly descended the stairs, pulling Jake with her. Mrs. Harrell started pushing Zachary and soon he was following his brother down the stairs.

Meanwhile, across town, Mikaela was frantically riding her bike through downtown. It would take her another ten minutes before she would be home.

Back at Arendelle Court, below the basement, a dim light illuminated a vast room that used to be the processing plant floor. It was over two hundred yards long with a long conveyor belt that extended from the original coal mine over to a large furnace. As they reached the bottom of the stairs, the boys were forced over to a giant furnace that had a small red glow emanating from it.

"You see boys, my plan is to take everyone in this neighborhood and dispose of them in this furnace, that way I get my neighborhood back." As Mrs. Harrell cackled with delight, Mikaela flew through the front door and passed her grandmother, running down to the basement. She had only been to the basement a few times and began to look around for where the boys might be. She could see stacked boxes and old furniture before finally spotting a small opening to walk through. She negotiated her way through the boxes and ended up toward the back of the basement. She could see the alcove and the door to the backroom. She immediately ran to the door and opened it. She saw the cot and other paraphernalia and then the open trapdoor. She ran over to the trapdoor and peered down, hearing the voices of Mrs. Harrell and Stella. She quietly slipped downstairs, holding on tightly to her backpack. As she neared the bottom of the stairs she hide behind a large post. She was horrified to see her brothers bound and gagged. They had been tied to the conveyor belt and Stella was about to pull a large lever to send them to their doom.

Mikaela moved to another post that was closer to the furnace, trying to not gain the women's attention. She looked around to see if there was a way to sabotage the conveyor belt. If Stella pulled the lever now it would be almost impossible to stop them from going into the furnace. Should she pull the box out now? She listened for Mother Light's voice.

"We come here today to celebrate the darkness," Mrs. Harrell said with an evil expression. She smiled at the boys, watching them squirm and struggle on the conveyor belt. While Mrs. Harrell seemed to be making some sort of incantation, Mikaela again snuck behind a post even closer to the scene. She could see that Mrs. Harrell was wearing a black ceremonial robe of some kind. Something she had seen in movies or pictures that depicted Satanic rituals.

"We plead to the darkness to return to us what is rightfully ours. We know that with the darkness we will be able to seek revenge. Death will come to those who have wrong the Harrell Family!"

When she finished speaking, Mrs. Harrell then walked over to the furnace. She peered in and could see a small red glow. She then pulled down on a lever that was attached to a large billow that went up and down and blew air into the furnace. Flames began to shoot up and Mrs. Harrell screamed with evil delight. She waved her hands up and down as if to signal the flames to rise higher. The boys looked down the conveyor belt toward the furnace and could see it's bright flames, giving it the appearance of a black dragon's face. It was horrible and they struggled all the more to try and get free but it was no use.

Mrs. Harrell then turned and walked over to a book that she began to flip through. She arrived at a page and then looked into the furnace.

"We pray to you Lord of the Darkness to bring glory to your name and destruction to all of your enemies. We commit the souls of these two boys to you and for your appeasement. Please restore the greatness of the Harrell name."

She then slapped the book closed and placed it on a nearby table. She looked toward Stella and then motioned for her to switch on the conveyor belt.

"Wait, stop!!!" Mikaela cried as she moved from behind the post. Stella turned to try and make out who it was.

"What are you doing here?!!!" a stunned Mrs. Harrell yelled.

"You need to stop this," Mikaela yelled back.

"Yeah, and you're going to stop us?" Stella questioned in a taunting tone.

Realizing she would never convince the women to stop their demonic intentions, she quickly pulled out the gold box from her backpack, but as she pulled it out she lost hold of it and it tumbled over to where Stella was standing. Mikaela raced over to retrieve it but Stella put her foot on it as Mikaela tried to get it back. Stella pushed Mikaela away and picked up the box.

"So what's in it?" Stella asked.

"Wait, don't open it," Mrs. Harrell implored Stella. "I've seen that box before. It's used by the people of the Great Light. There's a legend that the People of Light had talisman or objects they could wield that would destroy our people."

"Maybe I should throw it into the furnace then?"

Mrs. Harrell smiled and nodded. Before walking the box to the furnace, Stella pulled the lever on the conveyor belt and the machine, despite its age, roared into life. The boys could feel the vibration of the conveyor belt engine starting to push and grind and then finally go into gear. Like in the days of old, the conveyor belt was now working smoothly and moving its cargo steadily along. Mikaela, half-way between the conveyor belt lever and the furnace, hesitated as to what she should do. Should she run and pull back the lever or should she run after Stella? She looked at the boys. Jake and Zachary silently pleaded with Mikaela to save them.

"No, you can't do that!!!" screamed Mikaela. As Stella walked to the furnace with the gold box, Mikaela began to think about Mother Light and asked her for help. She looked around her and tried to find something, anything to throw at Stella. She found a small broken piece of brick and quickly threw it at Stella, hitting her in the head.

"Ow, what the hell!!!" Stella yelled at Mikaela. As she was hit, Stella dropped the gold box. Mikaela then ran over to the conveyor belt lever and pulled back on it. The conveyor belt shook and seemed to groan like a living creature but then heaved a heavy sigh and then stopped. Jake was just a couple of feet from being fed into the furnace.

With the boys somewhat out of harm's way, Mikaela resorted to her days of playing soccer. She started to run toward Stella by the furnace, but rather than sliding in to make a tackle like on the soccer field, she slide and scooped up the gold box, just in time, grabbing it away from Mrs. Harrell who also was trying to retrieve the box. As soon as she grabbed it, Mikaela opened the box and like a bolt of lightning, the room was immediately filled with a great, pulsating light that knocked everyone to the ground. Everyone in the room felt as though they had been flung to the bottom of a waterfall, feeling as though they were being pushed down by tons of water, but it was actually the force of the light. As the light began to pulsate more and more, just like at the hospital, the walls, floor and ceiling began to shake violently. Everyone was stunned and unable to move. The structure was quite old and it felt like it would soon crumble. Dust began to fly everywhere.

As the energy continued to shake the room, Mikaela had the presence of mind to get to her brothers. She untied them and told them to run upstairs. The boys complied with her instructions and were soon gone. Both Mrs. Harrell and Stella seemed transfixed and in a trance. The energy of the light was removing the darkness from their souls. When told, Mikaela closed the box and the room immediately returned to its original state.

As the energy in the room flowed away, Mrs. Harrell and Stella slowly were revived. They began to look around the room and at themselves. They studied their hands and arms and the rest of their bodies. They realized that they had been in a dark trance, controlled by forces from another world. Mikaela looked at them and realized they had a different look to them; a look of peace and happiness. They had been set free.

"Mikaela, you freed us. We were under a spell, a spell of darkness and you set us free," Mrs. Harrell said with great joy. Stella nodded her head in agreement. "Mikaela, please forgive me for how I've treated you," Mrs. Harrell pleaded with tears of joy. From upstairs there came the noise of multiple footsteps; Nanna Jean, Charlie and the boys ran down into the processing plant.

"What is this place?" Charlie said in his now usual stunned self.

"This is the coal processing plant and mill that the house was built on top of," Mrs. Harrell explained.

"I thought it had all been filled in with concrete to create a foundation?"

"That was the original plan but it was later scrapped in case they wanted to open the mill again."

Charlie and the rest of the children and Nanna Jean were all dumbfounded as they walked around the old plant floor.

"This place looks like it's hundreds of years old," Jake observed.

"Yes, it's from the origins of the industrial revolution, almost three hundred years old."

Stella walked over to Jake and put her hand on his shoulder. Jake was a little concerned that she might have other intentions and took a step back.

"Jake, I'm sorry we kidnapped you…I realize now we were under some sort of spell. Mrs. Harrell is my mother. I actually live down the street. We had been convinced that our land and property had been taken away from us but we realize now that it had been sold legitimately. Sold in time for us to get our house we own now because the family lost just about everything during the Great Depression," Stella said in a serene and calm voice Jake had never heard her speak in before. Mrs. Harrell put her hands around Jake's and Stella's shoulders.

"You should be grateful to your sister. She saved you."

Jake nodded and acknowledged his sister. He realized there was quite a bit to his sister than just a younger annoying sibling. He walked over to Mikaela and looked at her and smiled. He reached out to her and drew her close to him, giving her a big hug. Zachary and Charlie came in for a group hug and the family began to laugh. It was a laughter of relief. A laughter that released a massive amount of stress. Stress created by their mother's illness. Stress created from Charlie's unfaithfulness. Stress created from a spell that had controlled Mrs. Harrell and Stella. Stress created from Jakes adolescent foolishness resulting in drug use and other illicit activities. Everyone realized they had been given another chance to live in freedom, freedom from darkness.

"How's mom?" Mikaela asked her father.

"She is great. She wanted to come right away but the doctor's insisted she stay one more night. We will pick her up first thing in the morning."

As everyone walked back upstairs. Jake took Mikaela aside. He could see she was distracted by something. She was looking around the floor for the gold box.

"Something wrong Mikaela?"

"Ah, no. I thought I dropped something but now I can't find it."

"I want to thank you for saving me. That was pretty intense. I know you have been looking out for me and I really appreciate it. I realize now I was on the wrong path and you've helped me to see that."

"Of course. You are my big bro and I love you."

"I love you too and I will start looking out for you now. Although you probably don't need it."

"Just to have a relationship with you is enough. Anything is better than what we had."

Jake smiled and nodded. He knew that he had been given another chance and he needed to take advantage of it and he did. He later went to the university and later to law school. He had a large family and made sure he stayed close to his parents and siblings.

For Mikaela, she was no longer able to visit heaven. She had gone to the attic many times later but even when the sun was in the right spot, the portal didn't appear. She knew the reason why. Mother Light had told her that the portal would only be available for a short period until she had learned what she needed to know; to follow the light, avoid the dark and to help others. To not take oneself too seriously. To not prize wealth above everything. To help those less fortunate and to not focus too much on oneself.

Mikaela later married Billy O'Connell who had become a doctor. Mikaela was a stay-at-home mom. It wasn't what she had to be or settled to be but what she wanted to be. She could have done anything she wanted. She had graduated from college with a degree in biology and she would use that to educate her children which she had five of. But she didn't settle for that life, she enjoyed and loved it.

Zachary later became an engineer like his father, working for the city of Arendelle Heights. He married his college sweetheart and they had six children.

Stella eventually would go to art school in California and started her own interior design business. She married and had three children. She often came home to visit her mother and the Royaltons.

Mrs. Harrell would become a pillar in the community and a local historian, working at the history museum that McCaskey and Lund eventually built. She remained very close to the Royaltons.

Years later, the three Royalton children remained close to home and they stayed close to the light. Their mother Jayne had made a complete recovery from her cancer and decided to stay home full-time. The Royaltons lived happy lives and for Mikaela and Zachary, they would always remember their trips to heaven.

THE END